DATAMAN

A Mystery

by
Tom Mitcheltree

A Write Way Publishing Book

Write Way Publishing
10555 E. Dartmouth, Ste 210
Aurora, CO 80014

First Edition; 1998

Queries regarding rights and permissions should be addressed to Write Way Publishing, 10555 E. Dartmouth, Ste. 210, Aurora, CO, 80014

ISBN 1-885173-52-0

ONE

"Come on, you stupid shit. You ain't gonna get caught. Who'd be out on a shitty night like this?"

A boy cautiously emerged from the shadows. He was dressed like the other teen, wearing a black Raiders Starter jacket and a black cap to match, the bill swung to the back of his head. This meant the boys were about to do some "business." Business could mean anything from dealing drugs to a drive-by shooting.

"Let's go. We gotta show those fuckers."

The second boy looked around. Although in the middle of the city, the high school they approached was set in the open, surrounded by a wide expanse of playing fields on two sides and parking lots front and back.

"Javier, I don't like this. The last time we got in deep shit with the principal, we did this. They're gonna figure it out one of these times."

Javier walked back to Raymundo and spit near his feet. "These dumb fucks can't tell shit from piss. Come on!"

He swiveled around and faced a low brick wall that stood near the front of the building on which were large, brass letters: FREMONT HIGH SCHOOL. He pulled out a large can of spray paint from a pocket inside his coat, and with a great deal of care, outlined the name of his gang, 84th STREET, using letters large enough to eclipse the name of the school.

"This blue paint's good shit. They won't miss it when they come to school tomorrow. You got the red?"

Raymundo looked around nervously. He didn't know why he felt so scared. A thin fog rose from the grass around the building, making it hard to see anyone from the street, but they could still see any cops coming in time to make a dash for the playing fields. From there they'd have a dozen ways to get away and another dozen places to hide down by the football stadium. Even on a clear night, the chances of them being caught were slim.

He pulled the can of red spray paint from his jacket and waved it at Javier. "What do you want me to do with it?"

"I'll do some Crips on the front of the building; you do some Bloods. We'll fuck with their heads good."

Raymundo waited until he was around the corner to mumble under his breath, "Yeah, and if the Bloods find out we do this, they more than fuck with our heads."

Javier moved to the front of the building. The high school was made of a red brick, old enough so that it had a rough finish—perfect for spray painting. The only way they could get the paint off was to sand blast, and the sand blasting just made it better the next time they painted.

"The principal will shit bricks when she sees this," he said, smiling as he stepped back to admire his work. "You gotta see this," he yelled to Raymundo. He listened for a response but heard only a strange sound instead. He cocked an ear. "What the fuck ... You drop a watermelon over there or what?" Still nothing.

He walked slowly to the edge of the building and listened again. "Hey, Raymundo," he whispered. Raymundo didn't answer.

"Shit," Javier said. "He's probably painted himself around back." He edged to the corner and cautiously peeked around it. He couldn't see Raymundo.

"Hey, man," he whistled, "that's pretty cool." He moved away from the building so he could admire Raymundo's artwork. Above the low hedge in front of the wall Raymundo had sprayed BLOODS in bold letters about two feet high. What had caught Javier's attention was one of the O's. This one had a strange halo to it.

"How'd he do that?" He walked back to the wall. He still didn't get it. The halo was darker and mixed with other colors. This was new for Raymundo. He was good with a spray can, but he wasn't that good. He stepped through the hedge to touch the wall.

"I don't know what the fuck this is," he said rubbing his fingers together. "It almost looks like ..."

That's when he saw Raymundo, stretched out on the ground near his feet. Only it wasn't Raymundo. There was a big black hole where his face should be. Javier could feel the panic coming up from his chest. He felt that first surge of adrenaline. He even managed to look up and stare off into the mist.

Then the sound of another melon dropping echoed off the building, and another halo appeared around the second O. And then two bodies were stretched out between the hedge and the brick wall, both of them missing big chunks of their heads.

TWO

They call me Dataman. It's not a term of endearment. If anything, it's an accurate description. I am the owner, the manager,
and the soul employee of Dataman Investigation and Information Services. I am a resource. They call Dataman, Inc., from the
Mayor's office. They call Dataman from the police department.
They particularly call Dataman from campaign committees.

Big and small businesses call Dataman. I'm a resource to
universities and newspaper offices. Occasionally, as was the
case this morning, I get a call from a private citizen. They all
want the same thing, and they all pay the same price. They
want information, and I charge $60 an hour for it.

That may sound like highway robbery, and in a way it is,
considering I don't take polls, or run surveys, or accost people
on the street about their opinions. I spend most of my time
surrounded by computers that do the work for me. I'm a
subscriber. I subscribe to data bases from government agencies, from major businesses, from pollsters, and from other
information services. I get the data on disks and CD ROMs. I
have tons of software carefully labeled, filed, and stacked
around my office. I've got two computers connected to on-
line information services. I'm tied into an electronic bulletin
board that can get me information on everything from the

volatile mushroom trade to snuff movies. If you want to know something, chances are I can find it for you.

Sixty bucks an hour might seem like a lot, but you'd have to see my office. I've got ten different computers in it, each humming a tune of its own. I draw so much electricity that the cops stopped by once to make sure I wasn't using artificial lights to grow marijuana in the back room. Electronic toys cost a lot. Feeding them data costs even more.

That's the reason so many government and police agencies come to me. I always have the latest equipment. I can get the job done the fastest. If you know anything about government services, they upgrade their computers about every five or six years. By the time they're done, the equipment is damned near obsolete. I upgrade yearly, each time increasing my capabilities. In the end it's easier to come to me and pay me $60 an hour than it's to go to the expense of upgrading. Even the police come to me.

That doesn't mean they like it one bit. In fact one detective in Portland, Wilson, thinks he hates my guts. He doesn't. He hates technology. He loves old-fashioned police work. He hates the changes I represent.

Sometimes being Dataman works in my favor, financially. The fellow who called this morning wanted information about traffic accidents at a corner near his house. He wants to petition for a stoplight. I had thirty years of records for him in ten minutes. I still charged him for an hour. That helps to make up for those times I've sat at a computer for eight hours and couldn't come up with the info requested. No info, no fee. That's my policy.

What's it add up to? I've got a two-room office, one an apartment with a shower, on the second floor of an old, brick building in downtown Portland, Oregon. The building's in good repair, and I'm on the nicer side of the river. I've got a car that's paid for. I make the child support. I've got the world by the balls.

Of course, I live in the back room, I shower in the bath-room, and I eat at the cafe down the street. I've got some money in savings, but I never know when I'll need to up-grade one of the computers or shell out a thousand for a data base. It's okay though, because I'm my own boss.

Besides, you never know who's going to walk through the door next with something interesting for me to do. That's the best part, the variety. One day I might be reviewing some computer records to see if someone has tampered with them; the next day I might be asked to do some research for a mur-der investigation.

Because I don't come cheaply, folks don't come begging unless they really need my help. That means my work is usu-ally challenging. If it had been easy, my customers would have done it themselves. And my work is often rewarding. I've tracked down runaway children for the parents, reunited long-lost rela-tives, and even found money people didn't know they had coming to them.

Sometimes the work is not so rewarding. Sometimes the missing child turns up dead. Sometimes the long-lost relatives don't want to meet. Often I find more debts than money.

Today I have to call a family-owned business and tell the patriarch that his favorite son has been skimming money from the company and doing a poor job of covering it in the com-puter records.

Computer crime is not for amateurs. That's why I like it the best. That means I get to go up against the best. Give me a good computer scam any day and I'll be in my element. I love these things. I love the glow of the monitors, the rattle of the keys, the weird rumbles and the beeps and the power. The power to sit in my favorite chair and reach out to touch the world.

THREE

I don't usually see cops standing in my doorway, even when they have business for me. First I get a phone call, and then I get a written request. Mostly I'm asked to send over the results by messenger or to fax them. The check always shows up, usually a month or two late.

"Detective Curry," I said, to be sociable. Dave Curry was the Portland Police Department's misfit. He was a computer nerd who wore a badge and carried a gun. To be honest, he'd have a tough time finding either one in an emergency. The badge was in a suit coat pocket someplace, wherever he happened to throw the coat when he walked into work. The gun was in a holster clipped to the small of his back. The only time he seemed to notice it there was when he leaned back in a chair, which was almost never. He was one of those guys doomed to sit on the edge of his chair and stare intently into a computer monitor for the rest of his life.

He made a slow tour of the room, stopping at each of the computers to admire the screens, gently running his fingers over the keyboard until he dumped the screen saver and could see what was running. He didn't have much to see. I booted the machines up to menus, only running a program when I needed it. The rest of the time screen savers swept the monitor with spotlights, or flying toasters or changing works of art.

He stopped in front of my desk. I actually have a desk without a computer on it. It's where I eat when I get take-out.

"Tom."

"Dave." I didn't bother to offer him a hand, and he didn't look like he expected one.

"I might have some work for you."

"Might" was a big word for Dave. He hates to give up on something and turn it over to me. He does it, though, because he's overworked and under supported. The city believes in technology, which explains Dave's position, but it doesn't believe in the huge expenditures which goes with it, which explains why Dave still carries a gun and runs around investigating cases.

He should be back at his computer doing what he is about to pay me to do. Only, he doesn't have the kind of equipment I have, and when he finally gets it, I'll have better equipment. He's a smart man. He knows it's better to pay me to do some research that would take him four times as long than to work twenty-four hours a day. The city also knows it's cheaper to pay a consultant for two hundred or so hours of work a year than it's to hire another cop like Dave, or to upgrade computers as often as I do.

To stimulate the conversation, I said, "Yeah."

"I've got a requisition for ten hours of your time." He pulled out a folded piece of paper, unfolded it, and floated it down to my desk.

I read it. The numbers were right: ten hours at $60 each. Easy money so far considering the req. didn't say what it was for. I gave him my best, "Yeah."

"Two kids got blown away a couple of weeks ago."

"Yeah." This might sound a bit repetitious, but so far I still didn't know what he wanted and I didn't feel like fishing.

"We need some info."

I read the paper carefully each day. I've got headline news on one of the monitors with the volume down. I watch any news story or feature story that might give me an idea for more info, so I've kept up on the story. Two Hispanics killed while in the act of doing artwork on the side of a school. The news was hot for three days, and then it went to the back pages. The paper ran out of things to say, and the cops were not exactly vocal on this one.

"What kind of info?"

"You tell us."

We looked at each other for a long time. There wasn't much communicated in the exchange, more like a test of wills. Which one of us would be the first to admit the instructions were a little vague?

I cracked first. Six hundred was six hundred. "What have you got?"

Curry moved to the windows that overlooked the street and stood there in profile. From no matter what angle you saw him, he didn't look like a cop. Everything about him was soft, from the baby fat that surrounded his body to his voice. He was handsome enough, in an intelligent way, with his wire-rimmed glasses, his white-teethed smile, and his clear blue eyes, but he just didn't look like a cop. You could take the pocket liner out of his white shirt pocket and he still wouldn't look like a cop.

"Two dead teens, he said.

"Yeah."

"That's it."

Even I know better. "You've got to have more than that."

"We wouldn't be coming to you if we did." He said it like

he wouldn't be coming to at all if he could just walk off with a few of my computers.

"A bullet?"

"Pieces."

"Caliber?"

Dave made a slow tour of the room again while he gave my question some thought. This was curious considering it's not a question that needs much thought.

He completed the tour back in front of my desk. "I can't tell you," he said.

I gave him a Bronx cheer as I said, "If you don't want to tell me what you've got, I doubt I can help you."

"I doubt you can help, anyway. What we've got is some lead, home-poured for a slug. The slug was hollowed and the tip cross-cut. We're guessing thirty-thirty or a thirty ought six."

"You can't tell by the weight?"

"These were nasty slugs. They made a big hole going in; they made a canyon coming out. We're guessing the guy knew what he was doing. The slug flattened to punch the hole and then shrapnelled on the way through and out. We don't know if we've got all the lead. We only know one victim was missing a face and the other the back of his head." Dave shrugged. "Really, that's about it."

"What'd you get from the shooting site?"

Dave smiled. "What shooting site?"

"You've got to have a shooting site."

"Nobody heard anything, nobody saw anything. We found nothing but two dead teens."

"Nothing?"

"I wouldn't be here if we had something."

"You're talking a rifle fired in a high-density neighborhood, not once, but twice."

"We're talking two bodies not found until a Monday afternoon when the custodian finally got to the wall to scrub it. Despite the fact that maybe a couple of thousand folks walked, ran or drove through the area after the shooting. You'd expect more than nothing, wouldn't you?"

I began to see the problem. Still, it's hard to imagine not one piece of evidence that would be useful. "You've got to have something."

"Look, I don't need a lecture from you. This is Wilson's case, and I've had a lot of lectures from him. And we've both had lectures from the chief. And the chief has had his share of lectures from a small but vocal Hispanic community that wants to know why nothing is being done."

I nodded my head. Curry's not one to lose his cool and Wilson is not one to request my services unless they really didn't have much to go on. "This is gonna be tough."

He reached into his pocket and pulled out a short stack of newspaper clippings. He tossed them on my desk. "What you read here is what we've got. Nothin's been held back because there's nothin' to hold back."

I could see I might lose money on this one. I might spend a hundred hours on it without finding a thing. No info, no money.

Dave seemed to read my mind. Sweeping his hand around the room, he said, "This fancy pile of electronics probably has access to the information that will solve this crime, but I doubt if you will do any better than we did. Count on it."

"So why bother asking me?"

"Tom, on this one you get your money whether or not you come up with one thing. Wilson is looking forward to telling the media that even the hot-shit Dataman couldn't come up with something." He laughed, and then he turned and walked out of my office, saying on the way out, "That's the one thing I like best about you, Tom. Wilson dislikes you more than he dislikes me."

I was tempted to fax a quick no-thank-you to the police department, but then I stopped. There was a hell of a challenge dropped in my lap. I started to think of what a solution to this crime would do for business. When you're self-employed, good for business carries a lot of weight.

The elation only lasted a few seconds. The difficulty of the task began to slip in. If the shooting was random, the chances of finding an answer were impossible if there really weren't witnesses or clues.

The first thing I did was go to the one computer I had hooked up to the city. I paid a small fee for the feed to a basic data bank. This wasn't exactly hot information, but, surprisingly, it brought in a lot of dollars. I had access to schematics for sewer lines, power lines, water lines, etc. I also had access to detailed city maps. I was often asked by contractors to map out underground lines before they began digging or asked by neighbors to tell them something about property lines. Sixty bucks to me often saved thousands in legal fees or damaged water lines.

I pulled up a map of the city around the high school. After reading through the newspaper accounts again, I fixed the spot on the map where the bodies were found. I then did a quick cross-reference and brought up my ace in the hole. The city regularly took aerial photos. By keeping detailed maps showing outlines of building for each neighborhood, they could compare these to the photos. Should someone try to add a wing onto the house without a building permit, the city would know about it in time.

I put the map and the photos side by side on the screen. I learned immediately that a witness was unlikely at best. A large, grassy area separated the side of the building where the bodies were found from the nearest street, which was a four-laner. Houses on the other side backed to the road, didn't front it. That section of road was lined with back fences. I then checked the weather bureau records to confirm what I remembered about the night of the shooting. It had been a dark, cold, foggy night, not one in which many residents would have been out walking their dog.

That didn't explain why they hadn't heard anything. The wet air and fog would have absorbed some of the sound, but a rifle makes a big noise. Looking at the aerial photo again, I made a guess, one the cops probably made, too. The grassy area between the school and the street was a soccer field. A parking lot ran parallel to the field and the street. I would guess the killer parked there.

Did he shoot from there, too? That was a tough one. Even though there was outside lighting around the building, I didn't know if he could have seen clearly enough through the fog to make a shot. On the other hand, if he'd walked across the field, he'd have risked leaving foot prints on the damp grass and earth around the field. He'd have no way of knowing if the bodies would be found two days later or ten minutes later.

Which raised the question, did the victims see the killer? They were both shot in the head while standing up. One was facing toward the wall. One was facing away from it. Neither of them tried to duck or to run. A rifle that big probably had a bolt action or a lever action. After seeing your buddy's head explode next to you, you'd want to do something in that three to four seconds it would take to reload and aim. Except both were shot just standing. The police said in the newspaper one gun, one shooter.

This was an interesting puzzle. I could see I was going to be tested. I could also see I was up to the challenge. The killer obviously thought he was just going to be dealing with cops. He hadn't taken Dataman into account.

I went back to the desk and sorted through the work I had to do. I was looking for two child support deadbeats and a missing teen. I was pretty sure I could find all three by noon. I left the map up on the computer so I could get some street names, and then I set up another to run through a city directory and pull the names of everyone in the neighborhood and print them out.

I set up a second computer to print out all the hunting licenses issued for the last ten years. I did a quick program modification so no social security numbers were duplicated on the list. That would give me one clean list of hunters.

I set up a third computer to give me the names of all the students and staff at the high school. When I got all the lists, I'd scan them into another computer with a data program that would sort and match. By the time I was done with that, I'd have a list of folks in the neighborhood and school with hunting licenses. Next, I'd run a check of sales for rifles that could have been used for the shooting, with the list of hunters. This list, of course, would not be complete. I might not find a record of many of the rifle purchases, but I'd have a starting point and I might get some new ideas.

Curry was right about one thing: The answer to almost anything anyone wanted to know was in these information-rich computers. The name of the Green River Killer was here. The truth about Whitewater. The answer to whether or not a conspiracy killed the Kennedys. But you only get the right answers if you ask the right questions.

I didn't have time to worry about it now. I still needed to save a guy from the IRS tax court by trying to salvage vital data from a disk he left sitting on the dashboard of his car on one of those freak hot days we get in early spring. And then I've got to investigate some property for a hotshot European racer who fell in love with the area when he was here last summer to race in the Portland Indycar event. Then, the highlight of the day, will be to track the pedigree papers on a poodle that a client wants to purchase.

Being Dataman is about as romantic as it gets.

FOUR

I'm not native to Oregon. I'm a migrant non-worker. That is, I lost my job in the Silicon Valley in California just about the time my marriage was falling apart. I moved north where the living was cheaper and the computer industry healthier. My family stayed behind. I worked with Hewlett-Packard for a couple of years, long enough to pay for the luxury office complex I call home.

I would have starved to death in California trying to do what I'm doing here. Portland was just computer naive enough when I started to make the business work. Others have tried after me, but there's nothing like being first.

Right now staying first seems to be my biggest problem. If I don't come up with something good for the cops on the double homicide, the bad publicity could make me second.

By the time I faxed the info on the deadbeat fathers to the attorneys, I had a pile of printouts to go through. I'd also printed out a composite photo montage of the area and pinned it to the wall. My plan was to put names on the photo of anyone in the neighborhood who showed up on my list.

The list of names I got wasn't as long as I thought it would be. Only two names showed up on the list from the neighborhood, and only twenty students and faculty members had hunting licenses. That may come as a suprise because everyone from outside of the state thinks of Oregonians as being the great outdoor adventurers, but this is Portland, a large metropolitan area. The adventurers live out of town.

Instinct told me my sample was too small and the chances of the murderer popping up on this list was remote. I would check out the information I had, but already in the back of my mind I was looking for another way to approach this.

I knew I wouldn't give up until I couldn't figure another way to go at it. I suppose there are cops who pursue a case with emotional zeal to see justice done, or lawyers more interested in the principle than the money, but I could only name one or two. I wasn't particularly interested in justice or money. Like all hard-core hackers, I was interested in truth. Truth for us is the highest score on the arcade game, the answer to the puzzle, or, in this case, the name of the murderer. If it's in our computers to be found, we'll find it.

I suppose a moral issue is involved, too. When two Hispanic gang members get blown away while defiling a public building, again, I'm not sure how much empathy I can feel. Not much for two kids who chose a lifestyle that led to such things, though I can feel sorry for the parents. I can feel sorry for the community that has this much wrong with it. I can feel sorry for mankind who has yet to elevate himself above violence and vengeance, but basically I feel that two misguided kids acted in a senseless way and paid a senseless price for it. I *am* curious about the person who did it. If he were a gang member, that would explain a lot. If not, then the possibilities are endless—and fascinating. I'd like to solve this case just to find out who this killer is.

A man who works alone has far too much time for philosophical ruminations. Fortunately a woman walked into the office before I took on the issues of world peace, beauty, and the existence of God.

I moved to the front of the office where the desk is and greeted the woman at the door, offering her a seat in one of the chairs I have there.

She was an attractive woman, well-dressed, well-manicured, and well-coiffered. It takes money and time to have all those 'wells' attached to a discription. I've never been much impressed with good-looking women with money who have time on their hands. I like to see busy hands doing good things for neighbors and friends.

I offered her my hand. "Tom Walkinshaw. I'm Dataman."

"Margorie Whitlock," she said, shaking my hand with just the tips of her fingers.

Up close, a little of the attractiveness faded. She was polished here, buffed there. In the end, though, she was a classic sports car restored to pristine condition. Gorgeous at first glance, but dated nonetheless. I guessed that she was pushing forty.

"What can I do for you?' I asked.

"I want you to find my ex-husband. Can you do that?"

"I can usually find anyone, as long as he doesn't mind being found, or not old enough or bright enough to know how to hide."

"My former husband is both old enough and bright enough to know how to hide, and he definitely does not want to be found." She glanced around. "Do you have an ashtray?"

"I'm sorry, but I can't have smoking in the office. The equipment in here is sensitive, even to smoke."

She seemed to accept the excuse—with a show of displeasure. "Then let's make this quick. My husband disappeared six months ago, and he hasn't paid a support payment since he left."

"Support?" Divorce laws in Oregon are pretty liberal. Joint property gets split down the middle. Child support payments vary, based on the ability to pay. Spousal support is sometimes awarded if one party has a better ability to generate income than the other, but the support is of a certain duration, usually long enough for the spouse to get more education and improve his or her earning power. Alimony is rarely granted.

"My husband had a lucrative law practice. I fought for a part of it to be paid to me in monthly installments stretching over ten years. He had some investments that were to be sold eventually and split with me. He owes child support payment of five thousand a month."

My, my, I thought. Five thousand a month would buy a lot of manicures. "That's a lot of money for child support. How many children do you have?"

"Just one. A daughter."

"Her age?"

"Eight." I don't know if I raised an eyebrow or what, but she added quickly, "We decided late to have children."

I took a pad and pencil out of a desk drawer and began to take notes. "Give me the basic information, please, beginning with when he left."

"I really do need a cigarette for this," she said.

"Fine," I said. "There's a restroom down the hall."

Considering the look she gave me when she walked out the door, I wasn't sure she'd return. I wasn't too concerned. I had a good business and I didn't need her.

Still, I had to fight that urge to run out the door and beg her to come back. Starting a business like this, especially in a city where it had never been done before quite in the same way, had been harder than hell. The first couple of years I had prostituted myself setting up computers for people who didn't know a thing about computers. I was out every night in someone's home, installing, fixing, upgrading, rebuilding, or explaining computers. More often than not I had to go back a dozen times to add something new or fix something old. In the end I met a lot of people who turned out to be good referals for Dataman. In time I got out of the in-home business, which is good because a few more have gotten into it since. The bottom line is I have a good business which earns more than enough money for me. I don't need Mrs. Whitlock.

Just as I came to that conclusion, she returned, looking if anything better polished than when she left. Sitting back down, she started talking while I scrambled for the pad and pencil. "The divorce was granted a year ago. Shortly afterward, my husband began divesting himself of most of his holdings, including his partnership in the law firm. Six months ago he took the substantial amount of money he'd accumulated and disappeared."

"I'm surprised you didn't have something in the divorce decree that would keep him from selling out his holdings without your signature."

"William is not one to give up what he has taken a lifetime to accumulate. We never thought such a clause would be necessary."

"What about his daughter? He'd have to be pretty heartless just to walk out of her life."

"Yes, he would, wouldn't he?"

That seemed to be the end of that conversation. "Okay," I said. "This is what I need from you: a list of his relatives and the addresses you have for them; a list of his friends, close as well as business; I need to know where he went to school and when he graduated so I can see if he's contacted some long-lost classmates; a list of his credit cards and their numbers;

and I want to know the titles of any magazines he's subscribed to in the past. That will do for starters." Ignoring the blank look on her face, I wrote down the list on the pad and handed it to her. "Oh, I'll also need to know the name of the lawyers who handled the divorce for the two of you."

"He represented himself."

"Then your lawyer."

She rose slowly. "It seems like I'm doing all the work."

"If I'm going to find him, I need to start someplace."

She neither nodded nor smiled. She folded the piece of paper and put it in her purse. "When do you need this information?"

"I'll need it before your money runs out, or neither one of us is going to get paid."

"I don't appreciate your sense of humor, Mr. Walkinshaw."

"A lot of people don't," I said. "But it's the only sense of humor I have."

She turned and departed, leaving me with a little flick of her fanny to remember her by.

Beyond my first impressions, I didn't know what to think. Deadbeat dads were usually men with few resources and lots of vices, not men with lots of assets and successful businesses. They didn't have to run away. They could afford powerful lawyers who could get them what they wanted.

Somewhere in all of this Mrs. Whitmore was leaving something out.

FIVE

"... and for other local news this evening, police sealed off a train tunnel under the I-5 freeway in east Portland last night in what they called a sting operation to crack down on taggers. Four teens were arrested inside the tunnel, each carrying pack sacks filled with spray paint cans. For a report from the scene, we turn to Marva Ellis:"

"As you can see behind me, the whole interior of this quarter-mile-long tunnel has been covered with graffiti. It has become one of the favorite spots for taggers because it's seldom used and is left unsecured. In an interview earlier today, East Precinct Captain Dwayne Baker explained why he decided to run his sting operation:"

"We cannot go on forever letting kids deface our city. If we don't do something to stop them now, we're going to start looking like Chicago or Detroit. We want to keep Portland the livable city that it's."

"Thank you for that report, Marva. Railroad officials announced this afternoon that the inside of the tunnel has been painted over and gates will be placed across each end of the tunnel to keep out taggers. We must explain here that the tracks running through the tunnel are not part of a main line, but instead are routes from one railroad car storage area to another. Stay tuned and we will bring you a look at the local weather ..."

I turned off the radio, thinking it was strange to make a big deal out of covering up graffiti that no one could see anyway. The radio, of course, is an FM card in one of my computers that picks up the audio for local television broadcasts. That way I can hear what the local TV stations consider hot news without going to the trouble of watching it.

I was just getting ready to shut down for the night when my office door opened. A good-sized man walked in. I put him at maybe six four and two-twenty. He appeared to be in pretty good shape for someone who was past fifty at least. He had a bit of an awe-shucks, hayseed look to him, but the styled hair, buffed fingernails, and expensive clothes told another story.

"Evening," he said. "Wade Stewart." A big hand engulfed mine and abused it a bit before letting go.

"Wade, I'm Tom Walkinshaw."

"You the Dataman guy?"

"Yes, I am."

"Then you're the one I want."

He sat down on the corner of my desk, leaving me to stand or sit in one of my client chairs. I chose to sit. "What can I do for you?"

"Got a bit of a problem. Actually, I've got about fifty thousand bits."

I smiled. "That's a problem with a lot of parts," I said.

"No," he said. "It's a lot of bucks. That's how much somebody wants from me to keep from messing with my computer system."

"What do you mean by messing with your system?"

"I mean like wiping out my data."

"You mean someone is blackmailing you, threatening to destroy your computer records?"

"Isn't that just what I said?"

I'd heard of this happening in Europe, but I personally hadn't seen anything like it here. A blackmailer would threaten an on-line company with destruction of records, or sabotaging incoming orders. The threat was real enough as several successful blackmailers had proven, causing companies hundreds of hours of grief, lost records, and irate customers. More often than not the blackmailers were paid off and systems were then made more secure.

"I've heard of that happening before, but not in Portland."

"I'm not exactly excited about setting a precedent. What do I do about it?"

"One way of dealing with it is to disconnect your computer from the phone," I said.

He slapped his hand on the desk top. "I'm not about to do that. I just spent a small fortune going the whole hog, on-line orders, e-mail, a web page ... It would cost me a bundle to undo that now, and, besides, business has taken a leap since."

"Exactly what is your business?"

"Sports clothes. Casuals. Shirts, shorts, slacks: we're the one with the little skunk on the polo shirts."

A cute little skunk, too, if you happen to be three. I like the shirts, but I always take the skunk off with an Exacto knife. Nike, Pendleton, Jantzen: Oregon has its share of apparel companies. "No, I don't suppose you want to go off-line. Besides, it's probably too late."

"What's that suppose to mean?"

"It means that imbedded in one of those electronic orders you took was probably a virus, one your system won't detect, that can be triggered by the blackmailer."

"But if I'm off-line, how can he trigger it?"

"He or she, we're liberated in the computer industry. You might take in an order by mail and log it into you computer. Buried in that order is a certain sequence of digits and letters—probably the requisition number—that will start the virus working its malicious magic."

"So what do I do?"

"Pay the fifty thousand."

"You got to be kidding. My lawyer upstairs said you were some kind of hot shit and that's the advice you give?"

"Thank your lawyer upstairs for the referral, and ask him if he would be a little quieter in the mornings."

He stood up and put his hands on his hips and then leaned down toward me. "I don't get it. That's really all you can think of?"

"No. I could suggest you go to the police."

"I was told if I went to the police he'd let go with the records. The only reason I agreed to come down here was I figured he'd think I was at my lawyers if I came to this building."

I slowly raised myself from chair, forcing Wade to step back. "Paying him is the best way to keep him from destroying the records, although it's no guarantee. But if you pay him, someday he'll be back. Finding enough companies in this area with fragile computer systems to make this work for very long is tough. He'll eventually come back to you to see if he can make it work again. Doing nothing will get your records destroyed. Going to the police will get your records destroyed and a remote chance of getting him caught. Hiring me will probably still get your records destroyed and only marginally improve the chance of catching him, if he's smart."

"So what would you do?"

"Do you backup your records to tape?"

"Of course. We need some protection in case our hard drive crashes."

"Get the tape out and put in a new one. Backup your files every day, each day to a new tape. Stall the man and send me your tapes, especially the ones with records for the last six months."

"Why so long?"

"Because a smart man would have imbedded the virus months ago to make it harder to catch him. Now, next, I'd buy another computer system set up just like this one so that if the virus is activated you won't be off-line any longer than it takes to switch over. When you get that new system, make sure you copy nothing from the old one onto it. Once it's ready to go, call me. I'll install some safeguards to make it damned hard to do this again."

"Why don't we just do all this now?"

"We could, but we wouldn't catch the guy. Do you want to catch him?"

"You damned well know I do."

"I'll go through the tapes and see if I can find the virus I'm sure is there. I'll do what I can to salvage the data without triggering the thing and then I'll copy it to a new tape. Your records should be intact and ready to load onto the new machine. I cost sixty dollars an hour, plus the cost of any programs I use. I won't know how long it'll take, but I'm pretty sure I can save you fifty thousand dollars and save your data. I don't know if I can catch the guy."

He stuck out his hand again, laughing as he did so. "You got a deal."

"What's so funny?"

"Between the blackmailer and the lawyer, you're dirt cheap."

"You're right," I said. I too smiled while I shook his hand, but in the back of my mind I was praying the blackmailer wasn't better at this than me.

SIX

"Damn it all, anyway!"

The two boys stood in front of high, wire-covered gates that blocked the entrance to the railroad tunnel. Even in the dark they could see the gates rose high enough to cover the arch of the tunnel.

"Maybe we can crawl under them."

They soon discovered that crawling under them wasn't going to work, either. Railroad ties had been anchored into the ground on each side of the tracks, perpendicular to the tracks, and under the gates, to keep that from happening.

One of the boys examined the lock and chain that held the two gates-halves together. He said, finally, "I've got an idea. I'm going to climb up to the top of the gate, and when I yell, I want you to pull back on the gates as far as they'll go."

The other boy wasn't quite sure what his buddy was up to, but he knew if it could be gotten around, his friend could do it. He had tagged in more places than anyone in the city.

The boy nearly let go of the gates when his friend's backpack crunched to the ground near his feet, on the inside of the tunnel. Seconds later the other boys scrambled down the fence.

"Nothing to it," he said. "There's enough flex at the top

for you to squeeze over the fence. I'll push the gates out while you climb over."

Inside the tunnel, the boys moved to its center. Each opened their backpacks and pulled out an electric lantern. These lights were little more than a battery back with a rotating lens that stood high on one end so it could be adjusted easily. The boys had covered the lenses with blue gel one of them had stolen from their school's drama department. When the lights were set in place, the blue light bathed the tunnel wall with just enough illumination for them to see what they were doing, but without enough light to attract attention. From a distance the light looked like moon-glow. It was the perfect light for taggers.

"A fresh canvas," the first boy said. "They're going to be so pissed when they see this. I don't believe they had the balls to go on the news and say this tunnel was now safe from taggers."

"What shall we do?" the other boy asked.

"The cops know your tag, so maybe you'd better use someone else's. On a virgin wall like this, you don't want to risk giving yourself away. Throw in a couple of anarchy symbols and a couple of gang names to confuse them. I'm gonna do a giant Speeder, one like they've never seen before."

The second boy had to admire his friend. Not only was his artwork creative, but his tag, Speeder, was one of the best known in the city. He'd been so clever about leaving it, the cops still didn't know who he was. In fact, only the two of them knew who Speeder was. That's why his friend had never been caught.

"Bondo" had been caught because he couldn't keep from bragging. He'd gone out one night when Speeder couldn't get free and tagged the football stadium. No one had caught him in the act, but someone he'd bragged to narced on him. He'd denied everything when they pulled him in, and, of course, they couldn't find any proof, but from that day on he was on file as Bondo. That made it hard for Speeder because the two of them couldn't tag together unless it was someplace already covered with graffiti. Speeder didn't want to get linked to Bondo. Too many people knew they were friends.

Both boys opened up their backpacks and pulled out the cans of paint inside, lining them up in the order they would use them. The paints weren't cheap, either. Both boys used the best brands, ones that wouldn't run on them and ruin their designs.

Getting the paint was harder now. Most stores refused to sell the paints to teenagers, so they had to pay someone older to buy it for them, or they had to go to the black market. More than one gang had found that it was as profitable to break into a hardware store and steal spray paint as it was to rip stereos out of cars.

Speeder stopped what he was doing to watch his friend. He wanted to make sure his buddy wasn't going to leave his tag and get them both in trouble. Bondo was just finishing work on an anarchy symbol, the bold outline layered over a foggy-white surface. No one did anarchy signs as good as his friend.

Speeder started to turn back to his own work when a flash of red caught his eye. He turned back, fascinated as he watched a pin-point of red light dance its way up his friend's body. The light stopped on Bondo's temple and then held steady for several seconds. Then the light was gone and so was Bondo.

Speeder blinked. The image was still there, sharp, like something he'd seen in a movie once when this guy tested a dumb-dumb bullet on a melon. The melon had exploded in a shower of spray and small pieces flew through the air. Bondo's body had disappeared into the shadows of the tunnel before the spray had begun to settle, spotting the anarchy symbol and then drifting off in Bondo's direction.

Speeder turned to stare down the tunnel in the direction from where the red light must have come. On the ground, maybe fifteen feet away, the red spot reappeared. Speeder watched it as it moved toward him, moving around his feet, before flicking its way up his body. He saw it move up his chest before it disappeared from view. He knew he should do something, but he didn't know what. This was too unreal. He lifted the spray can, almost as an afterthought, and pointed it toward the end of the tunnel. Just as he pushed its button, he, too, died.

SEVEN

Henry Wilson was not a Henry, he was a Hank. Everything about him was raw-boned and rough-edged. Even with a smile, which I must admit I've only seen once, Hank is not a very friendly fellow. He's got the look of a brawler, and the sneer that's a regular part of his features doesn't distract from the image.

Today he looked much like he had the last time I saw him, only a little older and, if I wasn't mistaken, a bit concerned. When I saw him a year before he'd smiled when he told me that the police department would never use my services again if he had his say. Two dead Hispanic gang members might give him indigestion, but two dead white boys guilty of little more than tagging was sure to lead to an ulcer—and to my door.

Lieutenant Wilson shut the office door behind him and walked over to the one luxury in the room, a good recliner set near an open office window and across from a good boom box stereo with a CD player. He made himself comfortable in the chair. If I'd given him a cold wine cooler and put on a Maura O'Connell CD, he could have been me.

"You got my report, Lieutenant?"

"Six hundred bucks bought us a pretty term paper, all nicely wrapped up in an attractive folder and complete with print-outs of maps and other goodies. Of course it didn't get us a killer, so it wasn't a very good investment."

I suppose I should have my feelings hurt, but I don't. They pay for what they get. Given enough clues and enough time and enough money, I could find the name of the killer in one of my computers. I do know it's in there. Getting it out is the trick, kind of like getting the money you win at solitaire out of your computer.

"Pretty reports make your superiors feel better about the money you spent getting them."

He ignored the observation. "I read it. Now tell me what I'm suppose to have learned from it."

I swiveled around in my marvelous, high-back, padded desk chair, and gave myself a shove in his direction. I glided silently across the floor and then swiveled again at the last second and came to a halt facing the lieutenant a few feet away. This was a pretty impressive maneuver, and he should have appreciated it, but he didn't give a sign he had.

"No carpets on the floor, and only one chair for all these computers. The chair lets me glide back and forth between them." I waited a couple of extra beats to give him one more chance to be impressed. I could have waited a lifetime. "I see you want to talk about the report," I said, only a little discouraged.

"Like I said, I read it."

"Okay, let's give you the short version. This is what you know and I know together from the information you provided me and from what I found out on my own. The shots that killed the two Hispanic boys were probably from a thirty ought six, a pretty common hunting rifle in the northwest. No shell casings. The slugs themselves were too fragmented to give you much information. The best bet is that they were poured at home, hollowed out and cross-cut. They made a big hole going in and a big mess coming out.

"Your killer parked in parking lot next to the soccer field. He probably walked about halfway across the field, far enough to obscure him from the road and close enough so he could see the taggers through the fog. He used a night scope and some kind of a home-made silencer for the gun."

The recliner klunked forward. "Wait a minute. What makes you think he had a home-made silencer?"

"I thought you said you read the report."

"You mention a silencer in the report, but not a home-made one."

"Your analysis of the slug fragments show traces of foreign metal. Unless your taggers had metal plates in their heads, those traces have to come from somewhere. A commercial silencer wouldn't leave metal traces. Something fashioned in the basement at home would."

"How do you know what our analysis showed? I didn't give you that information."

I smiled the sweetest smile I could. "The information showed up on my computer screen, kind of like the Pentagon papers showed up on the *Washington Post*'s doorstep."

"You broke into our computer?"

I held up my hands, turning them over so he could see they were empty, and then I pushed up my sleeves so he could see I had no cards up them. "It was all done with mirrors. I didn't break anything, and I never left my chair, so I couldn't have entered."

He leaned back in his chair. I knew what he was thinking. When he got back to the station he'd make a big deal about how their computers weren't secure. He might be right or he might be wrong. I wouldn't know. I broke into the lab's computers.

"What else did you find out?"

"I doubt that your shooter lives nearby. Even in the dark of night and in the thick of fog, most folks don't put on a Rambo outfit and head out the door with their favorite hunting rifle. Family might ask questions, and if not family, the neighbors. I'm guessing the shooter drove to the site in a vehicle big enough for him to change into some dark clothing, put together his toy gun, and slip out without being seen. I'd look for a man with a four by four and a hunting license—unless, of course, he lives nearby and walked."

"Which takes you to the list of names I gave you. Twenty students and faculty members and two neighbors. The odds of your shooter being one of them is one in one thousand eight hundred and eighty-nine."

"One in one thousand, eight hundred and eighty-nine?"

"Long-shot odds. The case, as of now, has too many variables to it. In a case like this, those aren't bad odds, but they won't catch your killer for you."

"Since you are doing a lot of guessing, what's your guess about the killer?"

Just then my Siamese cat slipped through the window and jumped up on the back of the recliner. Hank leaned his head far back to see what it was, while Buck leaned far over to see who was sitting in my chair. The two of them stared at each other for a moment, and then Buck took the initiative. He licked the lieutenant on the forehead. He is not a discriminating cat.

The lieutenant rubbed his forehead with two fingers and then looked at them, expecting to find I do not know what. Both of them apparently satisfied, Buck stretched out on the top of the chair and the lieutenant directed his attention back to me.

"That's Buck. He takes the ledge to the fire escape, and

the fire escape to the roof. I keep his cat box up there. He likes to prowl for pigeons, but for the most part he looks for sun to stretch out in. He's been fixed. I thought when it came time to retire I'd get fixed and head for the roof."

I could see, just by his expression, that the lieutenant didn't joke much, and not at all about anything south of his belt.

"Like I was saying," I returned to the topic at hand, "I think your killer is a kook. Gang members don't go to that much trouble. They just spray the neighborhood with Uzis. He's working alone and he doesn't talk about what he does. If he did, you'd have heard some kind of rumors by now. Portland is not that big of a city. And, guessing from the latest news, he's serial."

Bingo! I got my second smile. "I kept telling those hotshot, information highway little shits, that you were a waste of time. Just like you, this new breed of digitized cop thinks the answer is in a computer and not on the street. We're talking gang, we're not talking kook."

He has a nice enough smile, and you really can't catch the venom in the tone of his voice, but his eyes almost went crosseyed in glee saying this, so it was pretty clear this was some kind of a told-you-so visit, only I wasn't privy to the other end of it. Apparently Hank has a problem with technology. If it was with spray cans, I could see him pulling the trigger on these taggers by the look on his face.

"Gosh, lieutenant, how could I have been so wrong? Gee, gangs. I never thought of that."

"Why is it every jerk they give a computer to turns into a smart ass?"

"I don't know about the others, but I always try to sit on a good book when I'm working on my computers." I was right the first time. No sense of humor about anything south of the belt.

"The second shooting was in retaliation for the first. Two spics got it the first time. Two honkies paid the revenge price."

I'm always glad to find that racism plays no part in police investigations. I knew I should keep my mouth shut, but Poe's Imp of the Perverse had to go someplace when the story was done, and he turned up on my shoulder to whisper in my ear things I should never say out loud. "I think some progress has been made in gang relationships," I said. "I'm talking real progress. It's neat the way they're now sharing weapons."

"What's that suppose to mean?"

"Lab report says all four were shot with the same gun."

"The lab report's not in yet."

"It's now."

He glared at me for a long time, turning just a shade pale while his hands trembled a bit. Buck didn't like it and left through the window. For a second I was afraid I might follow him against my will.

Hank stood up slowly and hovered over me for a second. "I know there's something we can nail you with, just you wait and see. I know you've broken some law, and I'm looking forward to being the one to arrest you." He used his foot to give my chair a hefty shove. By the time he'd made the door, I'd done a nice one eighty and was back to my keyboard. I didn't bother to say goodbye. The look on his face said it wouldn't take much to push him over the edge.

I had to feel sorry for him some. The public didn't get too excited about gang killings as long as they didn't happen on their doorsteps. Serial killers were another thing, especially when they started bumping off nice white kids who'd advanced beyond finger painting. The lieutenant and his band of merry playmates down at the station were sure to feel some heat soon. For now the only thing left for me to guess was whether or not they'd want more hours out of me.

I had to feel sorry for him a lot because he was probably a good cop who was in the process of being passed by because of technology. Curry was the cop of the future. Wilson was the one due for pasturing. I doubt if anything could change the course of that future.

I didn't get much time to consider Wilson's fate. A brief phone call commanded me to go to River Place to pick up the information requested of Margorie Whitlock.

River Place is one of those up-scale condo clusters on the Willamette River right on the edge of downtown. Not only are the folks who live here treated to a nice view of the river, they have easy access to good restaurants, the performing arts facilities, and fitness clubs. This is where much of the city's mobile affluent have decided to park. If I had the money, even I wouldn't mind a condo down there.

Ms. Whitlock's condo was in one of the older, more expensive buildings. For $200,000 you could have a two-bedroom apartment facing the interior courtyard. For a heck of a lot more you could have the corner luxury flat with the panoramic view of the river and city, the one Ms. Whitlock had.

I was met at the double front doors by a maid, who escorted me through a gallery lined with expensive-looking paintings, to a large living room. I was given a few minutes to enjoy the view before Margorie appeared, wearing something off-white, flowing, and form-caressing. She looked quite lovely again, and in this setting, home, even more a forgery of youth than before.

"I've asked the maid to bring us coffee," she said, pointing to a sofa where she wanted me to sit. Once I was down, she placed a folder on the coffee table between us and sat herself. "This is the information you requested."

I picked up the folder but didn't open it. "Is there anything else I should know?"

She looked a bit alarmed for a second but then composed herself before asking, "Such as?"

"The reason for the divorce."

"That's none of your business."

I tossed the folder back on the coffee table, the action an intended message. "If I'm going to look for your ex-husband, I'm going to need to know everything that can help me. Things like whether or not there was a third party involved—we might find him through that third party."

She colored slightly. I was sure the idea that her husband might be cheating on her caused the anger. That's why I stated it that way. I wanted to find out what reaction I would get.

"I'm sorry, but there is no third party."

"I looked around the room. He gave up quite a bit considering how little he got in return."

"I'm the one who wanted the divorce. We were simply no longer a good match."

I was absolutely sure that I wasn't going to get a further explanation. I suppose it was the way her lips snapped shut and disappeared after she said the last word. Or maybe it was the way she glared at me. At any rate, she had body language even the blind could read.

I picked up the folder as I got up. "I'll see what I can do," I said.

"I expect results."

"My policy is that I don't charge a fee if I don't get the information you want. I also don't take on a case unless I think I can find some useful information. I'll let you know as soon as I find anything. If the case doesn't look promising, I'll return this information to you."

She nodded her head. "I understood that you were the best at this sort of thing."

"If I don't find your husband, you can turn it over to someone else and find out for yourself whether or not I'm the best."

I left, feeling we had both drawn so many lines in the sand that we left a pretty crosshatch, but neither one of us had made any points. Someday, when I haven't got one damned thing better to do, I'm going find out why people take an instant dislike for each other. I don't understand it one bit, considering she doesn't look a thing like my ex-wife and I don't look a thing like her ex-husband if the picture of him in the folder is a good likeness.

I came back into the office just in time to answer the phone. It was Wade Stewart, calling to tell me he'd gotten another e-mail demand for money. Shortly after, all the orders that had come in by computer that morning disappeared from the computer.

EIGHT

I don't know about other men who've gone through a divorce, but I know I was determined to learn something from it. Exactly what that new knowledge is hasn't become clear yet, but if I were to guess at it, I'd have to say it has something to do with not getting married again until I know for sure that's what I want to do.

I didn't get that choice the first time. I was twenty-two. She was eighteen, pregnant, and Catholic. We got married. I didn't consider it to be a shotgun wedding at the time, and I still don't. I loved the woman very much then; I probably still love her now. Only I never let myself dig deep enough in that pit to find out for sure.

I have two lovely children, fourteen and twelve. Neither is speaking to me. They used to come up here for the summers with their noses turned up in the air. Being with Dad in a hick state like Oregon was just about as much as their Southern Californian cool could tolerate. When the youngest turned twelve last summer, the ex went to court to have the visitation agreement canceled. The children didn't want to make the trip. The judge agreed. I learned about the court appearance three weeks after it was over in a legal document that said I still had the privilege of paying for their support, but I could no longer see them unless I came to California, took up residence nearby, and agreed to a Wednesday night visit each week and two Saturdays a month with my children.

I didn't agree. My business is now up here, as is my life. Why my ex would even want me back in California is still a mystery to me, unless she feels that a court system that seems to favor her might make me jump through hoops down there. She calls me occasionally and screams at me on the phone about how heartless a father I am, refusing to meet the needs of his children, the same children who won't talk to me when I call. She was sleeping with a friend of mine when I finally caught on. That wasn't the first friend she had slept with while we were married. I often wondered why I had so many friends.

We did it all—the counseling, everything. I learned she'd married too early, and felt she'd missed out on some of her youth, and that her infidelity was a way of capturing the adventure she had missed by marrying me. Not much was said about the fact that she told me she was on birth control when she got pregnant, or that I wasn't ready for marriage either, but I did it because it was the right thing to do.

Working long hours in a fledging computer industry is what we all did in the beginning. The competition was fierce and the rewards were grand for the few who succeeded in a big way. The company I was in succeeded in a big way at first, and then it got steam-rolled by complacency. I was left high and dry in a down-turn of the economy holding a big mortgage when housing prices collapsed. I lost a small fortune in the recession and most of the rest in the divorce. The only thing I kept was some stock in my former company. Right now that stock's worth a good chunk of money. My ex hasn't found out yet.

My day's about done. It's been a good one: I tracked down a dozen property owners for a builder who's looking for some locations to develop; I found the exact property lines for an owner who's having a feud with his neighbor; I traced some financial records for two divorce cases and for one political candidate; I did some research for the attorney general's office on court decisions involving benefits for significant others, meaning of course gay, lesbian, and common law relationships.

I also had time to cruise the net looking for information about homemade silencers. I found five articles, two for handguns and three for rifles. The simplest of the lot called for three cans of increasing sizes and some fiberglass insulation. Surprise, surprise. The trace of metal found in the lab report was aluminum. I then faxed the lab, using the police precinct address, to request a look for fiberglass fibers in the autopsies of the four shooting victims. That only took them two days. I just intercepted their latest report. Bingo. Our shooter apparently cruises the Internet, too.

My last operation of the day is to shut down all but one computer, doing a quick diagnostic check on each before putting it to bed. When I first started, I kept a large supply of computer parts in the storage closet just in case I found something wrong. Now I just keep three complete new computers still in their wrappers in the closet. When one of these goes bad I simply trade it in on a new one. I've got an arrangement with a dealer down the street.

I had just finished shutting down the last one when the office door opened and Dave Curry walked in. He wore slacks, a white shirt, a tie, and a sweater. His glasses suggested too many years of eye strain staring at a computer. He didn't have a pocket protector today, but he had a pocket computer organizer instead. His hands were soft. His complexion was pale. His body was pudgy. I had looked like that once until I came up here and got a limited membership in a health club down by River Place. I play city league basketball three times a week during the season. We organize pick-up games three days a week the rest of the year. The pudge disappears in a hurry playing full-court ball with guys who like to run.

"I want to talk to you about the tagger killings."

Tagger Tragedy. That's what the Oregonian had called it in a big headline after the second shooting. The name had stuck. Green River Killer. I-5 Bandit. Hillside Strangler. You've got to have a good name when you are dealing with serial crime. The only problem was that everyone wanted a serial crime but the cops.

I shoved my computer chair in the direction of the detective and moved over and sat down in my recliner. As he sat down, I decided he must be one of the "little shits" that Wilson had mentioned. "Right," I said, "the taggers. I think the official police report says that you guys believe the shooter is from a rival gang and the shootings have something to do with turf. Let me see, now. Since we have dead Anglos and dead Latinos, that makes the shooters either black or Asian, although I guess it could be bikers, druggies, rednecks, or a secret police assassination squad."

He smiled. I liked him the first time I met him because of his sense of humor. He swiveled slowly in his chair, noting the details of each computer and the peripherals attached to them. When he turned back to me, he said, "Impressive. That's the first of the new Pentiums I've seen. How many megs?"

"Sixty-four megs in that one. I use it primarily for graphic-intense information."

"And the other ones?"

"When they go bad, I replace them with the fastest computer I can afford."

"The luxury of private enterprise. You'd be surprised how

many four-eighty-sixes we're still using. Most of the Pentiums we have aren't up to the tasks we need to do."

"Lieutenant Wilson must buy your computers for you."

"He wouldn't buy us an abacus. We're assigned to the same division, but he's not my boss."

"I bet that the good lieutenant is the one promoting the gang theory."

"It's his theory, and, since those who disagree with him are considered to be technicians instead of police officers, his theories carry more weight than ours."

"I see," I said, glancing at my watch. I wasn't trying to hurry Dave along, but I had to meet Stewart this afternoon, talk to Ms. Whitlock, and be done in time for a tech rehearsal at the theater.

I do tech work for a community theater group. We jokingly call ourselves the off-Broadway group. We are precisely three blocks off Broadway, the central thoroughfare through downtown Portland. The Performing Arts Center is on Broadway. I've done some work for them, too. When a big show comes in to Civic Auditorium, I get hired on to help set up and run the computer controlled lighting and special effects. I've worked most of the big road shows including *Cats, Phantom of the Opera*, and *Les Miserables*.

Somehow, working those shows takes something out of the enjoyment of watching them. After you've seen Jean Valjean drinking coffee from a Styrofoam cup between acts and stood next to Jauvert at the urinals, the show's not the same.

Dave pulled out a folded piece of paper from behind his pocket computer and handed it to me. "We want some more of your time."

I unfolded what turned out to be a check made out for $1800. "Thirty hours, to be precise," I said.

"That's guaranteed. Should you come up with information that catches the shooter in less than thirty hours, you get to keep the whole amount. If you use up the thirty hours and we like your report, you'll get some more hours."

I stared at the check for a long time. Something wasn't right here. "Does the good lieutenant know about this?"

"The good lieutenant doesn't know how to turn on the computer on his desk. The city is making an effort to upgrade its computers. We technicians have a budget to operate out of. You'd be surprised how much of it's set aside for consultation. Not only do we want whatever information you can give us about the shooter, we also want a detailed account of how you went about researching it. We plan to study your research techniques and incorporate them into our department. Make sure you give us one of those 'pretty' reports, as the lieutenant calls them. We like them even if he doesn't."

"So you don't think we're talking gangs?"

"I think we're talking a psycho who's fed up with graffiti and has decided to do something about it. He's got enough money to own some pretty good equipment from night scopes to guns. He's smart. He's found out how easy it's to kill some folks that society doesn't particularly like anyway. He'll keep killing until he's caught."

"You're a pretty bright fellow, Dave," I said. "I'd bet you've got a hell of a computer system at home and probably one hidden away in the police station someplace. Why do you need me?"

He smiled. He said, "I don't have the time you have. I don't have the equipment. I can't hack my way into places I'm not suppose to go because I have a better chance of getting caught at it."

I looked at the check again. "I'm all yours," I said.

After the detective left, I grabbed my briefcase with my theater gear in it and took off out the door, making sure it was well-secured behind me and the alarm system was activated. Part of that security system was a monitor I had installed over the door. Anyone approaching my office would see themselves in the monitor. They could only assume that they were being videotaped, which they were. You'd be surprised how many people looked up into that monitor and then turned and walked away.

I met Wade Stewart in front of the KOIN Building. We'd decided that it would not be wise for us to meet at his office in case whoever was doing this was watching to see if the police showed up.

He handed me a paper bag. "All the things you wanted are in here. I'm getting ready to do the other things you recommended, but I don't want another episode of data being erased."

"Set up your tape backup system to record new data as it comes in. If you don't know how to do that, we'll arrange a time when it's safe for me to come in and do it for you. Actually, I want to set up the new equipment for you anyway, so I can do it all at once."

He looked a little older and a little less confident than the first time I had seen him. "Why me?"

"You're vulnerable," I said. "You're new to computers and don't have the safeguards that more experienced or bigger companies have."

"I'm beginning to wonder if I should have gone to the police."

"That's a choice you can make," I said, "but let me tell you that the police often come to me for help. They just don't have the resources that I have. If they catch the guy, it won't be through the computer. Although they might get him when he tries to get the money."

"He wants the money wired to him."

I thought about that for a minute. "That's clever," I said. "He could arrange for that wire to be forwarded a half a dozen times. Electronically, we could track it, but I doubt if we could go at the same speed as the wire. He might be able to get the money and be gone for hours before we found out where he picked it up."

"Are you sure?" He sounded dejected.

"I'm just guessing. But I'll do some research and get back to you."

"I thought I had a good chance of fighting this until I found out the records had been erased."

"This is the computer age," I said. "Crooks are inventing crime faster than we can imagine it. If I can find a way to stop this guy, I might have a way to stop a thousand guys who try it after him."

He nodded his head and walked away, thinking I knew not what. I didn't have time to worry about it. I had a definite need to meet with Ms. Whitlock to discuss a piece of information I had discovered.

I walked down to River Place and took the elevator to the top floor of Ms. Whitlock's building. The maid let me in. Margorie Whitlock was waiting for me in the living room, standing next to a window that cast a pale light on her features, making her complexion and eyes even more opaque than usual.

She didn't invite me to sit, but said, "I suppose you have something for me."

"Not yet," I said, "but I do have a few more questions."

"Such as?"

"Why you didn't tell me you accused your ex-husband of sexually abusing his daughter?"

She did not move, and maybe it was the fading light itself that caused it, but she seemed to turn white, even the pale blue of her eyes. "Does it matter?" she asked.

"It matters in several ways. It might explain why your husband has been so hard to find. He seems to have a reason to stay hidden. It explains why he hasn't tried to contact his daughter."

A hand came up and gently clutched one of the curtains, as if she needed the additional support. "No legal charges were brought against him. Reports from my daughter's psychologist were presented at the divorce proceedings, along with a medical report from her doctor. We thought the evidence was strong enough to discourage him from trying to get custody."

I was a little bit confused. "You had evidence that your husband abused your daughter, but you didn't want to bring legal charges against him."

Her fingers clutched the curtain. "The evidence was not absolutely conclusive. I didn't want to put my daughter through what would be a difficult ordeal if he were formally charged."

"So you kind of suggested that if you didn't get your way you'd take this evidence and make a big deal out of it."

Her head snapped around. "Fathers abuse daughters."

"Statistically, not as often as it's claimed," I said.

"It doesn't sound like you want my business."

"I agreed to do a job, but I can't do it if I don't know what I'm up against. People disappear for lots of reasons. How completely they disappear depends on the reasons they have for vanishing. If the reasons aren't too serious, they usually don't cover their tracks very well. If they have a good reason, they can disappear and stay disappeared."

"So now you think my husband is one of the second."

"I don't know," I said. "If he's afraid of being charged

with a crime and he has the resources, I'll never find him. If he's angry for being falsely accused, he might not have been as careful."

She turned her head back to stare out the window. "I need his support money. Find him."

I nodded my head. She wasn't conceding anything, but she still thought I could find him. That gave me something to think about. I left, letting myself out the front doors.

I ate a quick Chinese at the Metro and reviewed my notes for the play. We were doing *Noises Off*, a slap-stick comedy that had dozens of special effects that needed precise timing. Many of them I had programmed into the computer, those that turned off and on lights and brought up sound effects. Some of them, though, still had to be done by hand. Those were the ones I was reviewing. We are a small theater company. We have more actors than stage crew. When the play opens, I'll be running the booth myself. That's a bit scary. What's even more scary is I'm scheduled to direct *I Hate Hamlet* in the winter. I've never directed a play before, but the others think it's time I started.

NINE

According to theater lore, if dress rehearsal is a disaster, opening night will be flawless. Put that up there with marriage is forever and good is rewarded and evil punished. Fortunately for us, *Noises Off* is so full of intentional mishaps that the unintentional went by for the most part unnoticed by the audience.

I have three pages of notes for the director of things that went wrong. Most of them will be squared away by tomorrow's show, but by then the actors will have invented a few more catastrophes. One actor, I'm sure, will not try to put his fist through the wrong pane of glass again tomorrow night—instead of connecting with break-away glass, he hit Plexiglas. They say the sprain will heal in time. But the actor who picked up the phone after the first ring only to get her best laugh for the evening when the computer rang the phone a second time is desperate enough for audience response to do the same thing tomorrow night.

I shut down the lights after the crowd had left, satisfied that I did my part. The crowd wasn't bad for an opening night. It filled about half the theater. Actors take comfort in that. If they're going to blow a show, it's apt to be opening night, and if they blow one, they want it done in front of small crowds.

I waited backstage for Diane Jantz, the lovely actress who spends a good part of her time on stage in her underwear. She's a lovely creature and she's often cast in plays in which she is in her underwear. She took their breath away in *Butterflies Are Free*. She certainly has taken my breath away more than once.

Diane is a psychologist, complete with her license and a brand new Ph.D. She's twenty-five, blonde, blue-eyed, incredibly built, and gorgeous. If you ask her why I am the current love of her life, she will tell you that she is testing a theory of hers. The theory goes something like this: Since the advent of the computer age, women are now, slowly, shifting the values by which they choose mating partners. Before they sought out good genes, tight buns, and hips that suggested good thrusting power. Now they seek out the brilliant minds, the masters of the computer universe who will be the power structure of the future. Hey, if it gets her in my bed, who am I to question her theory?

I asked her, the first night she came home with me, if man was choosing his mating partners in a different way. She dropped every last stitch of clothing and got an appropriate physical reaction from me. "I don't think so," she said.

In my more jaundiced moments, I suspect our relationship will last through the end of my directing debut. She really wants the female lead in *I Hate Hamlet*. In part, she wants it because she'll get to keep her clothes on. In part, she wants it because she wants it. That, after all, is what drives most actors. That and the applause at curtain call.

Why else would they put in the hundreds of hours it takes to put together a play production? Rarely is it the play itself. While the audience sits on the edge of its seats, waiting to see what will happen next, the actors are usually backstage waiting to come on. How do they kill their time? They sneak out in the alley for a smoke. They tell each other war stories. They even read books or practice a tryout for another part. Tell them you'll record the play and give the tape to them free, and most will say don't bother, or, "just tape my parts." Few have a clue what the whole play is about, only his or her part. Why, then, do they do it? For the curtain call. For those few moments of recognition and applause.

Why do I do it? I don't get a curtain call. I do it because I need something that separates work from the rest of my life. I need something that is more creative and appreciated than what I do alone in my office. I need an activity that lets me meet someone like Diane.

She came out of the dressing room and paused a moment, posing with one hip thrust out and the opposite elbow high on the door frame. She likes to be admired, and she likes the way I admire her. She has her hair pulled back in a pony tail, and she's wearing a huge, white, cable knit sweater that comes to mid-thigh, over black tights and white sneakers. Even under that bag of a sweater enough curves show through to let you know this is one shapely lady.

She dropped her pose and pranced over to take me by the arm and drag me toward the stage door. We said our good nights to a half a dozen people and entered an alley devoid of fan fare. Amateur theater is healthy in Portland, but the actors don't take on star status. With luck they might get cast in a production at the Performing Arts Center. A good showing might lead to a season at Ashland's Shakespearean Theater. A few good contacts there might mean a chance at television or film. Don't give up your day job. Few have made the journey from our off-Broadway Theater Troupe.

"Ah, good," I said, "we won't need to fight our way through your fans tonight. I hate the way they grope me when we go through."

"If there were any fans, it would be me they would grope. You they would look at with a great deal of puzzlement."

"It's not my fault this thirty-six-year-old body has let me down. I said I'd treat it right if it would let me look like Tom Cruise. Face it, I don't look like Tom Cruise."

"Take heart," she said. "In twenty years Tom Cruise will probably look just like you."

Part of our endearing relationship was for me to allow her to practice witticisms. At my expense. I'm not allowed the same courtesy.

"You had a better opening night than the others," I said.

"They would have done as well if they could have taken off their clothes, too."

"No, dear. Take my word for it. They wouldn't have been able to pull it off." That was an understatement. We look specifically for scripts that keep our actors clothed.

We walked the few blocks to the Metro. On a corner near Pioneer Square, the Metro is located in the heart of Portland. It's no more than a ground-floor cafeteria with a selection of fast foods from Chinese to Greek, but it's the gathering spot of choice for the late-night crowd; it's cheap, and it stays open late.

Diane and I end up here after every rehearsal or show. More often than not, she takes a cab from here to her condo in the Portland hills. Occasionally, when God is very, very good to me, she walks the few blocks to my place. Born to drama, she rarely let's me know which exit she's going to take until she takes it.

We got coffee and moved as far away from the piano player as we could get. Anyone can sit down and bang out a note when the piano near the entrance is not in use. Tonight the player seemed to have decided he'd invent a rock'n roll version of free jazz.

Diane looked up from me and smiled. She had that freshly

scrubbed look of someone who had just removed her makeup. On her it was a lovely look. As our makeup artist put it, the only reason he used makeup on Diane at all was so the back row could see how beautiful she really was. "Why do you always look at me like it might be the last vision you'll ever get?"

"Fear that it might be the last vision I ever get." On most nights she had little patience for my insecurities. She didn't seem to understand that once a man had been with her, little after would ever be the same. Some woman would forever be playing second fiddle to her memory. I didn't fear losing her. I feared never being able to forget her.

She reached across the table and patted the back of my hand. "I'll tell you when you need to worry."

"That's comforting," I said, "but I have one question. Will you tell me before it's too late to do anything about it?"

She thought about that for a moment. "You know, Tom, that's a good question. I imagine if I felt compelled enough to tell you to worry, it might already be too late. On the other hand, a fairness factor would demand I tell you in time to change my mind. I guess the only way I could do that, is to tell you before you actually have something to worry about, which means I'd have to be a bit of a tease and jerk you around some, which means ..."

"Okay, okay, okay, I get the picture."

"Right now I'm a pretty content woman. There's no one else in my life as important to me as you, and I'm not looking for a replacement. Go with that. Every woman you love isn't going to betray you."

She likes to cut to the heart of my insecurities even though I don't. I know, deep down, that a failed marriage doesn't mean a failed life, but, on the other hand, having been so completely betrayed by one woman makes it very scary when I'm so desperately in love with another. I could probably go with it, as she says, if I wasn't so afraid I'd be devastated if I lost her. Only goddesses come in packages this complete.

I'll admire her, but I'll never let her know just how much I love her. That knowledge would be enough to scare us both. "Do you have time to talk shop?" I asked.

She got that little smile on her face that can just melt my heart. "I've got all night."

From the reaction on her face, I think I must have blushed a bit. She's rarely this obvious about her intentions. To gather myself together, I said, "Taggers."

The look turned quizzical. The marvelous thing about dating an actress is you get a variety of expressions that are easy to read. No mysterious looks from her. "Taggers?"

"I've been contracted by the cops to see what I can find out about these tagger shootings."

"You know," she said, pausing to sip her coffee, "there's an empty office in your building. I'm thinking that might be a nice spot to begin a practice."

She planned to start her career with a family counseling service. I'm a little skeptical about the potential for her success. The women who come to see her will be intimidated by her beauty, and the men will want her to share the couch with them. Still, it's not a very big building, and I can imagine some wonderful possibilities for the lunch hour. "That's nice," I said, "but what has that got to do with taggers?"

"What it means is, once my practice begins, you'll have to pay a consulting fee to get answers to your questions."

"We'll talk about that once you open your office."

"Fair enough. Now, what do you want to know?"

"What turns someone into a tagger?"

"One problem with the police is they want to find a simple answer for every question. You won't find simple answers here. Tagging may be an act of anger or an act of revenge. The principal expels you from school, so you tag the building. Your girl friends cheats on you, so you tag her car."

"This whole thing, the shootings, might just be a complex game of revenge?"

"Get me something to eat and let me think about that."

"What do you want?"

"How about a gooey pastry and some caffinated coffee. I'm going to want to stay awake, and I'm going to need a spurt of energy." The smile turned malicious. She knew how well she could work me.

I tried not to show that I was trembling as I got up to get something for both of us. When I returned a few minutes later, I noticed she'd written some notes to herself on a napkin. Some lines were followed by question marks. She was the type of person who would look for an answer if she couldn't come up with one. Because of her dedication, I doubted that she would fail at anything she tried in life.

Following the list with the tip of her pen, she said, "I don't think what we've seen so far is a pattern of revenge. The two sets of victims don't appear to have been connected with each other. The third party, the shooter, has singled out two different races in two dissimilar parts of the city. Tagging is sometimes territorial, much like a dog peeing on a tree trunk or fire hydrant. The dog is marking his territory. The tagger—often associated with gang activity—is marking his territory. Schools are almost never territories. The train tunnel wasn't a territory, either."

I had to think about that. The tunnel was in a part of town where gang activity was prevalent. "Why do you say that?"

"Gangs want their tags to be seen. The tunnel was for a different class of taggers. These are the artists. Tagging is a form of artistic expression for them, and they want their tags to be seen by other artists. The tunnel was a giant canvas."

"How do you know that?"

"I saw the pictures of it before it was painted over. Gangs paint over the top of each other's tags. None of that took place in the tunnel. This was a gallery in which each tagger respected the work of the other."

"Art, gang signatures, and revenge. Anything else?"

"Sure. The danger of it all. Tagging can be a dare-doing activity. You've seen tags high up on buildings or near the top of overpasses on the freeway. Someone put his life in danger to make those tags."

"Why couldn't it have been a her?"

"Female taggers usually fall into the artist category. In rare cases, you have girls doing gang tagging, but the risk factor makes it more of a male activity."

"Any other risks?"

"Getting caught. This is sort of like organized football for the disenfranchised. It's a game with risk, danger, and possible injury. Taggers get to test their manhood and their tags are proof for bragging rights."

"My generation didn't tag. Why now?"

"Your generation grew up with the involvement in Viet Nam. For all you knew, you'd get out of high school and go off and fight in the jungle. People got assassinated, city blocks were burned to the ground, mobs rioted, soldiers killed: You didn't have to manufacture danger in your life; life came prepackaged with it."

Sometimes I get a chill when the right buttons are pushed. I cry when I see tapes of J.F.K., even though I was only a child when he died. I can't see the black slash of a memorial for Viet Nam in D.C. without misting over. I can't watch movies like *The Deer Hunter* or *Full Metal Jacket*. In the end, I was too young for the war, but others I knew weren't, and some of them didn't come back. The years of it are as imbedded in me as they're in any veteran.

"What about the shooter? What do you think makes him tick?"

"I don't have an easy cop answer for that, either. More than likely he's a male, and he's crazy. We usually don't assign murdering people to the sane category. Yet, we might be looking at a sociopath instead of a psychopath. I haven't seen any reports that this is a crime that has happened in other cities in the same way, so I don't see a drifting serial killer doing his thing from place to place. My guess is you have a sociopath, one who appears to be normal to the people around him, who got shoved over the edge."

"What does it take to shove someone over the edge enough to start killing people?"

"In this case it's hard to tell. Someone might have tagged his new, four-by-four truck. Or, he might be a neatness freak, someone who gets frustrated because he can't keep up with the disorder in his world, and, tagging, for him, is the final straw. I'm afraid we won't know the answer to that one until someone catches him."

That was a depressing thought. How many more killings might it take for that to happen? The Green River Killer chalked up close to fifty kills without being caught.

She stood up and grabbed my hand. "Come on. Tomorrow's Saturday and I plan to sleep in while you make me breakfast in bed."

No taxi tonight, I thought. As we walked the few blocks to my building, I thought a little more about taggers, but to tell the truth, by the time I was fumbling with the keys to my office, I wasn't thinking about them anymore.

TEN

I bought my office space. The building I'm in is old, historic, as a matter of fact. As a result the historical commission in Portland insists that space in this building be purchased by each occupant. The idea is that a landlord can't be conned into selling this prime piece of real estate for big bucks so a new high rise can go in, and it would take all the owners to agree before the status of the building could be changed.

Regardless of everyone's motives, I'm glad to own the space. It has allowed me to decorate my two rooms to my taste, and I think I've pretty damned good tastes. The main room is sixteen by twenty-two feet. When I moved in, I scurried off to a small town east of Portland that was tearing down an old courthouse, from which I got the oak panels that line the room, and the oak railings that separate the entry from the rest of the room. I've a reception desk and very comfortable jury chairs on that side of the railing. On the business side are oak library tables with my computers on them, my recliner, and the judge's chair on wheels.

The ceiling is fourteen feet high and the two sets of double windows are twelve feet tall. The room is light, airy and comfortable. When a client walks in the door, he or she doesn't get the impression of walking into the den of a hacker. They get the impression of a first-class operation.

The second room is on the corner of the building. It's twelve feet wide by twenty-two feet, and it connects to the first by a door in the middle of the wall. This is where I was really clever. The bathroom, which is six feet by twelve feet, is on the end by the hall. Here I have a deep sink, a toilet, a glass enclosed shower, and an over/under washer and dryer. Next to the bathroom is a kitchen area I built in, complete with cabinets, microwave, and portable dishwasher. The washer is built into the counter next to the bathroom door and the extra long hose I installed reaches the bathroom sink. The kitchen area is separated from the front of the room by matching opaque glass panels and French doors, again both trimmed in oak.

The living room has double sets of windows on each side of the corner. Here I have a huge sectional sofa that goes around three walls, surrounding a massive coffee table. Also in the room is a round, oak dining table, closed so it can only seat three comfortably, and an expensive stereo system.

My pride, though, is the loft. I built it myself over the kitchen and bathroom. You have to climb a library ladder to get to it, and more of the courtroom railing keeps you from pitching into the living room. I have my bed, dresser, armoire, book shelves, television and VCR in the loft. It's great place to be on the weekends, since I'm the only one who lives in the building, but it's not quite so great after eight in the morning on a weekday. There are law offices above me, and one of my fellow owners has a pretty heavy foot-fall first thing in the morning.

It's a particularly nice place to be when I can wake up on a sunny morning with the beautiful Diane curled up in my arms as she was this morning. In fact, as she was for the last two mornings. This was the first time she had decided to stay the whole weekend.

She lifted her head and asked, "Where are my clothes?"

"They're on the floor in the living room."

"I didn't leave them on the floor down there."

"I know. I threw them over the rail."

She poked me in the ribs. "You did what?"

"I threw them over. You know how I like to watch you go up and down that ladder naked."

"You and anyone else who can see through those windows of yours. I must be one of the major attractions in Portland."

"You *are* one of the major attractions, but like I have said before, folks can't see through the curtains." My thin curtains let the light in during the day, yet they provided a great deal of privacy. I know; I climbed every building in the neighborhood to find out if I could see into the apartment through them.

"You're right," she said, climbing slowly out of bed and stretching so that all the curves of her body undulated in incredible ways. "That's really depressing for an exhibitionist."

Another theory she has. All actors and actresses are exhibitionists. I started to crawl out of bed after her. "Let me go down first."

She pushed me back on the bed. "So you can do what?"

"So you can exhibit for me while you go down the ladder."

"No way, buster. You got the whole show last night. No freebies today."

It didn't matter. She looked great going down the ladder from up here, too. I slipped into my bathrobe and climbed down after her. "Shall I fix us breakfast?"

"Give me a few minutes and then come in and scrub my back," she said, slipping into the bathroom. "After that, let's go to Powell's and eat fat food, drink Starbuck coffee, and read everybody else's newspapers."

"There's something cheap about you," I yelled through the door.

"I'm saving money to buy that office," she yelled back.

"I forgive you then."

Portland has more bookstores per capita than any city in the United States. Powell's is the bookstore supreme of this literate city. It rambles from room to room and up to down. In fact, it has rambled so much that parts of it have had to be annexed to nearby blocks of the city. At one corner of this institution is a coffee shop surrounded by two walls of windows. Here, on any morning of the week, one can sit undisturbed for hours and read magazines off the nearby racks or read newspapers left behind by the dozens of faithful who have gotten there before you. Add some chocolate brownies and two huge cups of coffee, and you have a morning that the two of us love to spend together.

We hogged a table meant for four and spread out several newspapers. Diane worked her way through the advertising, always looking for a bargain, although she rarely went shopping. She seemed always to be honing her shopping skills even when she wasn't using them. I started with the sports section and moved forward. Like most Portlanders, I was curious to see what the Trail Blazer basketball team would do next. The Blazers won the championship once in the 'seventies, and had come close two other times, but now they were in need of a serious rebuild. How they were going to go about doing that had everyone curious.

I flipped over one section of the paper to find the Meier & Frank ad, one that featured some wonderfully flimsy female underwear. Tapping the pictures, I asked Diane, "How come I can see through your underwear, but I never can in these ads?"

She picked up the ad and held it up to see. She announced, "Because these are very special women. They have neither nipples or pubic hair. That's why they get selected for these ads."

I only caught part of what she was saying. The headline on the front page dangling in front of me took most of my attention: TAGGER TRAGEDY CLAIMS ANOTHER VICTIM. I took the paper from her and placed it in front of me. "Damn," I said.

"What's up?"

"Number five," I said. "And he's not up, he's down. The shooter struck again."

She twisted around a bit to see the paper and then gave up, saying, "Read it to me."

I read: "'Seventeen-year-old Brian Clark became the fifth teen shot by a killer whose victims have all been taggers. He was shot in the head by a high-powered rifle while spray painting his tag on the side of a used bookstore in the Hawthorne District of Portland.'"

She found the same story in another paper and read the rest for herself while I finished the story. The kid, from what I could tell from the story, never knew what hit him. He pulled out a spray can and then he was dead. I wondered if the other taggers in the city would get the message.

"This is interesting," Diane said.

"Tragic is more like it."

She glanced up long enough to roll her eyes at me, and then said, "He wasn't alone."

"Who?"

"Clark. It says in here that he was with his girl friend. She was handing Clark paint cans and acting as lookout when he was shot."

I looked for the information in my paper and found it. After reading the part about the girl friend, I said, "She's lucky she didn't get shot, too."

"Lucky?" she asked.

Now I saw what she was getting at. "He could have just as easily shot her as the kid."

"Exactly. And why didn't he?"

"You're the psychologist. Why didn't he?"

"Get me more coffee while I think about it." Dutifully, I did just that and refilled my own cup while at it. When I returned, she had again written down a little list and was tapping it. As I put down her coffee, she said, "He could be a she, reluctant to shoot one of her own. I doubt that, though. If this were a gender thing, our shooter might be tempted to aim south of the belt. More than likely our shooter has a strong value system, one that says you either can't shoot females or says you can't shoot a tagger unless he or she is caught in the act of spraying a wall."

"That's what we like. Indiscriminate killers with high value systems."

"Not indiscriminate. So far, the shooter hasn't shot just anyone. My guess is he feels he's on a mission."

"To clean up the city?"

"I doubt if it's that simple. More than likely it's some act of revenge. For what I do not know. Find that out, and you'll find the killer."

Diane had a theory that women, who were catching up to men in cancer and heart disease, would eventually catch up in crime. She truly believed in equal opportunity for the sexes. "I did find a couple of hunting licenses issued to females in my research. I suppose I could go back and look at them if you think the killer really could be a female."

"I wouldn't waste your time for now. Serial killing is still almost exclusively the territory of men." She tapped her finger on the newspaper article. "The last paragraph is interesting."

I read it. It seems that Brian Clark had been arrested and prosecuted for a number of tagging incidents. His sign was well-known around the Hawthorne district, so much so that the police had set up a stake-out to catch him in the act. He was featured on the news being dragged in court, his mother standing in front of the cameras claiming that her son was being persecuted. I remember seeing the news broadcast. I don't remember her claiming he was innocent.

"I remember seeing that on the news," I said.

"Exactly," she said. "You saw that on the news, and you saw the piece about the train tunnel on the news. Your shooter must watch the news, too. How else would he find his victims?"

"That explains these last two incidents, but what about the two guys shot at the school? Neither the school nor the taggers had made the news before it happened."

She nodded her head. "Yes, I see."

"See what?"

"The school is the key. Something happened there to start this, something that didn't make the news, but something that got the killer's attention."

She did have a point. The police could not link the shootings to anything prior to the episode at the school. "I'll have to talk to the cops some more about the school," I said.

"Why don't you go there yourself and look around?"

I laughed. "I'm not a cop," I said. "Nor am I a licensed private eye. I can't just walk into a school and say I'm there to investigate a crime. I've got to have some authority."

"Call the cop who hired you. Get him to go with you."

The idea was interesting. I'd seen all those *Magnum P.I.* shows with Tom Selleck running around in Hawaii in his pretty red Ferrari. I wasn't as tall nor as good looking, and I had an Austin Healey instead of a Ferrari, but I could still see a relationship. Dataman, Inc., was an investigative service and a research center. I didn't call myself a private investigator because I had no interest in carrying a gun or spending my time outside someone's bedroom window trying to catch a husband or a wife committing adultery. "I'll call tomorrow."

"Let me know what happens." She was soon done with her coffee and off wandering the psychology section of the bookstore. I stayed behind and ran through my calendar for the week in my head. We had a matinee of the play this afternoon; I had several projects to finish up at work; and I had basketball games on Monday and Wednesday nights. We rehearsed Thursday night, and then we had three more performances. Tuesday afternoon was my best bet. I could get a few hours free. I'd have to see if Curry could find some time.

I arranged the items on our table to make a clear statement that we would be back, and then I went looking for a book or two in Diane's territory. I wanted to find out more about parents who molested their children.

I could have asked Diane about this, but she goes ballistic on the subject. Needless to say, she tends to shoot her rockets at the boyfriends or the husbands, although she once admitted in a moment of weakness that the mothers are sometimes co-dependents.

If I'd known from the beginning that child abuse was an issue, I wouldn't have taken the Whitlock case. This is one where the child always loses. If the father is guilty, the child is a life-long, damaged victim. If the accusations are untrue, if the child is a pawn in battle between parents, then the child still is a life-long victim, used by one parent to try to destroy the other.

I had no feeling about the case, yet. If a crime was committed, someone needed to report it. In Oregon, laws requiring that officials of any kind report suspected cases of abuse are pretty tough. No legal action was taken against Mr. Whitlock, which meant the case had to be very weak. So why did Mr. Whitlock run?

I returned to the table before Diane and buried a book I found in a stack of others that I was going to buy.

When Diane came back she paused a second to run a hand through my hair. "You're in luck," she said. "I think I have just enough clean clothes to stay one more night at your place."

"I must have been a very, very, very, very good boy," I said.

"You weren't bad, but I wouldn't want you to think you were that good. Where would be the incentive to try to improve? Besides, I've arranged to meet with a real estate agent to look at that office in the morning."

"That hurts," I said. "I thought you were interested in my body, not my building."

She sat back down and pulled out the comics from the pile of papers. "Just think of how much more time I might have for your body if I have an office in your building."

"I can't think about it," I said.

"And why not?" she asked, glancing over the top of a sheet of comics.

"Because I don't want to get my hopes up."

From behind the comics, she said, "That was just the right answer."

ELEVEN

Getting into Fremont High School would have been easier if I'd enrolled as a student. Getting in as a visitor takes an act of God. Detective Curry, in this case, got to play God. He could not join me at the school, but he worked behind the scenes to open the door for me.

Opening the door means getting past locked doors and a security guard. High schools today are kind of like prisons, as most high school students have thought at one time or another, only they lock the outside out instead of the inside in. In a neighborhood with gang activity and an occasional drive-by shooting, Fremont High is the King's X of the neighborhood. You don't get in the door unless you can get past the metal detector and the security guard.

When I arrived at the building and got approval from the guard, a secretary came down from the main office and escorted me to the principal. This had happened to me once or twice before, only I was a student then in a high school in California. I'd made the trip enough times I thought the principal and I should be on a first name basis. "Dick" suspended me for a week. It turns out his first name wasn't Dick.

Even going back to school for parent conferences with my own kids depressed the hell out of me. Walking in a school brings back such vivid memories, good and bad, from youth. It hurts too much when you realize how much you've out-distanced that time and how impossible it is to ever go back.

The principal in this case turned out to be an attractive black lady named Janette Cray. She shook my hand when the secretary introduced us, and I thought that I would never have it so good again in a principal's office. She motioned me to a seat across from her and then sat down behind her desk. A principal's desk is a little bit like a monarch's throne. When one sits behind it, there is no doubt who is in power.

Ms. Cray said, "You have the look of a man who hasn't been in a high school in awhile."

"When I last went to a parent conference, my kids were in grade school. I haven't been in a high school since I walked out of one with a diploma."

"Let me assure you this school isn't that much different from the one you attended. Many of the same subjects are still taught in much the same way. Kids here still cross the spectrum of humanity, many good, some not so good. Teachers still have varying degrees of competency. The rules still seem absurd, unless you happen to be running the place."

"That's comforting to know," I said. "Only I don't remember anyone getting shot to death on my school grounds."

The pleasant smile on her faded just a bit. "Probably not in your neighborhood," she said, "but maybe in some other neighborhoods at schools not quite as nice as yours."

"Maybe," I said. Deciding this could spiral down to a situation less than ideal for good communication, I went for tact. "Your school's got a pretty good reputation. Other than occasional vandalism and the normal nose-punching over a girl, you don't seem to have too many problems here. Did it surprise you that the two kids were killed while tagging on school grounds?"

"We do have a good school," Ms. Cray said. "We've had to work hard to get it. Police in the halls, metal detectors, unannounced locker searches, quick follow-ups to even a hint of a problem: We've done everything we can to keep this a safe environment. I won't try to fool you, though, because I understand you have access to just about any kind of a statistic that can be had. Our school boils beneath the surface."

I knew exactly what she meant, because I did have access to the statistics. Seventeen percent of the school population was Hispanic. Thirty-five percent was black. Another twelve percent was of mixed minorities. The majority population, then, was thirty-six percent of the school. Majority population. That was an ironic term assigned to whites outnumbered two to one by minorities.

"I've seen your population figures. I suspect you have both racial and gang problems. I'd also guess that not all the Anglos are pleased to be in a minority, and I can bet you get an earfull from parents on a daily basis, but when does all of that add up to murder?"

"According to the police this looks like a random act."

"Perhaps," I said, "but why did it start here? How did a serial killer, picking out targets at random, know he would find the first two here?"

"Maybe he was cruising and stumbled across those two."

"We're talking two o'clock on a dark, cold, foggy night at an isolated spot from surrounding streets. He couldn't have spotted these guys while cruising. He'd have had to get out of a vehicle and come looking for them. I'm not sure a man who's been so cautious as to shoot five people without leaving a clue behind, is going to go wandering around a school ground carrying a high-powered rifle, unless he's pretty sure he's going to find a target. This is where it all started. I think the solution to this crime is here."

She folded her hands on her desk and gave me one of the best condescending looks I have ever seen. "I think it's interesting you think that. I'll wait, fascinated, to see what you come up with."

"I appreciate your cooperation. I know it's late in the day, but I would like to have a chance to speak to some students today and perhaps a few staff members. Of course, I'll need to arrange future visits so I can interview more completely."

"You haven't talked to Detective Curry lately, have you?"

"No. Should I have?"

"If you had, you'd know I told him I really did not want you in the building at all. It has taken us some time to calm the student body since the first shootings. In fact, the second and third shootings have been a God-send. We've convinced the students that no one here is responsible for the deaths, that the attacks were random, and they no longer have anything to fear. You don't know how close we were to an explosion here. The gang the two dead boys belonged to believed that one of the other groups in school was responsible for the deaths. Those groups didn't like the notion that they were being blamed."

A little picture forming in the back of my mind suggested the resources available to this woman were not going to be thrown open to me. "And you're afraid an investigation by me might stir up some bad feelings?"

"You are a very perceptive man, Mr. Walkinshaw."

"What kind of cooperation can I expect from you?"

"Until I got a call from my superintendent, none at all. Now, as little as I can get away with."

"Doesn't that sort of fly in the face of what the police and the superintendent want?"

"The police and superintendent do not have to sit behind

this desk. Their careers will not be on the line if I have a gang
or racial explosion take place in this building." The smile was
gone, replaced by a full-blown, I-am-God-in-this-building look
I'd seen before, just before I was suspended.

"What can I expect from you, then?"

"I asked my secretary to put together a packet of information which includes a copy of our yearbook, issues of the
school newspaper, memos sent to the staff, announcements to
the students, a school profile of the victims, and my own
thoughts on the case. She will give that to you before you
leave. I am announcing to the students a number where they
can reach you should they think of something about the case
that has not been given to the police. In a few minutes, I'll
take you down to the library for a staff meeting and introduce
you. They, too, will be given your number and be encouraged
to call you should they think of something new."

"On their own time?"

"Of course. Teachers are far too busy to waste school hours
talking to researchers."

"I like to think of myself as an official investigator."

"You go right ahead and humor yourself."

A bell rang. Ms. Cray came out from behind her desk and
walked out of the office. I assumed I was to follow. She took up
a position in the hallway outside the administrative offices. I
noticed that the crowd of students shoving gleefully down the
hallway, anxious to get out of the building for the day, calmed
noticeably when they approached the principal. Although they
might jostle each other in their hurry to leave, an area around
Ms. Cray went unpenetrated by students. She didn't smile at
them, and they didn't smile at her. I understood then that she
was one powerful woman, and whatever crumbs she was willing
to throw me were all the crumbs I was likely to get.

As we walked down the hall toward the library, I asked her, "How long have you been principal here?"

"This is my first year," she said, a bit tight-lipped.

"What happened to the previous principal?"

"He was asked to retire."

"Too old for the job?"

"No," she said, smiling a bit, "too soft. He tolerated far too much from both the students and the staff."

"Would you like to elaborate on that?"

"Not at all."

We walked into a staff meeting that was ready to begin. Apparently Ms. Cray expected her teachers to be there on time, and apparently they all were. At least no one came in once we entered the library.

I had expected some preliminary business to be taken care of before we got to me, but I was wrong. Ms. Cray started the meeting with, "This is Mr. Tom Walkinshaw. He is the owner of Dataman, Inc., a research firm the police are using in the investigation of the Tagger Tragedy. I'll give each of you his phone number. If you have any information you would like to share with him, I encourage you to call."

I was still surveying the crowd when I realized we'd come to the end of her presentation about me. A few seconds is not much time to assess maybe eighty faces staring back at me. I only got a few impressions. I didn't see any smiles. Many of the teachers had the late spring look of veterans, that is, they looked like they suffered from combat fatigue. Only a few stared back at me. The rest looked infinitely bored.

Ms. Cray whispered to me, "My secretary will escort you out now."

I gave everyone my best departing smile, turned, and nearly ran over the secretary who was carrying a stack of things for me to take along. I was out the door and into the parking lot before I knew it.

I did get a chance, in the hall, to glance around. The building looked exceptionally clean, even for the end of the day. That said a lot, again, about the principal. The halls were nearly empty. No one seemed to linger long after the bell rang. I wondered if that was from choice or because of some kind of policy. Finally, I noticed how young the few students I saw seemed to be. I found it amazing that these children, so much younger than the young adults I went to high school with, could have so many adult problems, from pregnancy to murder.

After I put the materials in my car, I corralled a custodian who was lowering the flag out front and had him show me where the shootings had taken place. Seeing the scene first-hand was reassuring. I still thought the shootings happened the way I proposed they'd happened.

When I got back to the office, I found that a visitor had stopped by and left me a message. I've got a button next to the door with a sign over it that says to press and leave a voice message if I'm not in. Actually, the button activates the video camera so I can see the person leaving the message.

The message was left by Lieutenant Wilson. It was short, with appropriate facial expressions to go with it. He had said, "Datashit. I don't like people going behind my back, cops or civilians. Whatever new information you find comes to me before it gets to Curry. Have a nice day."

Inside my office I stacked the materials I'd been given into neat piles. One yearbook. Ten issues of the newspaper. A pile of notes and memorandums. One neatly type-written report on the shooting from the principal.

I wasn't ready to wade into this quite yet. I was still smarting a little from both Cray and Wilson. Egos, careers, status quo: all these things seemed to come before catching a killer. I was discouraged.

I walked back to the one mainframe I kept up and running all the time. I used this for a variety of things, including voice messaging when I was out of the office. The computer contained one message, a rather excited one from Diane. "Tom! I can swing the deal on the office. Only one problem: I have to sell my condo. Would you mind very much if I lived with you for awhile?"

Of course I wouldn't mind. And, yes, the whole idea scared the shit out of me.

TWELVE

"I won't be staying very long," she said, as she hauled into my office a box with her things in it.

"Why? Don't you think we can make it?" I asked, my insecurities shining through one more time.

She gave me that look and rolled her eyes. "No," she said. "I don't think it will have anything to do with us. What it will have to do with is the fact that living in your apartment is a bit like living on a sailboat. You just don't have a lot of room."

"I've cleared a couple of drawers for you and some closet space."

She laughed. "Boy, have you got a lot to learn. I need about as much space as your apartment just for my makeup and clothes."

I didn't know if she was kidding or not. I'd never been in her bedroom, as strange as that might sound. I'd been to dinner at her place a couple of times, but the nights we spent together were either here or at a hotel when we went away together to someplace like the beach.

"I could try to make some more room for you," I said.

"Don't bother," she said, carrying the box into the apartment. "Although my office isn't as big as yours, it does have two rooms. I'm using my living room furniture for the front part of the office for now. I'll use the back room for storage and keep my things there."

That made sense. It would be some time before she could afford a secretary, and most counselors now had offices that resembled living rooms. When she came back out of the apartment, I said, "I wasn't expecting you quite so soon."

"Are you having second thoughts?" she asked.

"Third, fourth, and fifth, but I haven't changed my mind."

She stopped for a moment to look at the papers on my desk, the ones from the school. "Having second thoughts is very healthy," she said. "So are third, fourth, and fifth. If things are not working out for us, we'll both know it, and we'll both do what we have to do."

"Do you need some help carrying anything?"

"Nope," she said. "I've some clothes on hangers to bring up, which will take just one more trip. After that I'm going back to pack up. You probably won't see me again until this weekend."

"Can I help you pack?"

"Not without confusing me. If I do all the packing, I'll know where everything is. I'll need your help moving over to this building on the weekend."

"When you make up your mind, you make up your mind."

"Being broke helps. I used all my savings as a down payment on the office. I need to get the condo sold as quickly as possible, not only to pay off the office, but also to have some cash to get started in business."

For a long time I was left to wonder about Diane's finances. She lived in an expensive condo, drove a BMW, and didn't work except to go to school. I guessed she was independently wealthy. I was only half right. Her parents, who have a good deal of money, gave each of their children a substantial bequest when they got out of high school. The message they gave the kids was very clear: Do what you can with this money. When it runs out, you won't get anymore. We are leaving the remainder of our estate to charity when we die.

Diane lived well while going to college. She did a good job of managing her money, so much so that she'd make a profit on the condo when she sold it. From what I knew of her, she would be a success as a counselor the same way she'd been a success as a student, and a success as an actress.

In some ways my parents had done for me what hers had done for her. Except they died doing it. My mother died prematurely of cancer. My father followed not long afterward of a classic broken heart. He died in the middle of my divorce. What was left to me from their estate helped me get out of California with the shirt on my back. It was their money that bought my office. I would trade it all to have them back again.

Diane stopped in the doorway and stared at me for a long time. Finally she said, "I can't believe it. I'm going to be living with a man."

"How are your parents going to take it?" She explained to me once that the reason we didn't stay at her place was that she had neighbors who were nosy, and I had no neighbors at all. Her mother was the type who'd introduce herself to Diane's neighbors and then casually ask each of them if her daughter had any men spending the night.

"Dad will have a heart attack and mom will have a stroke. Other than that, they'll handle it just fine."

I used one of her psychologist tricks. "And how do you feel about that?"

She walked over and flicked the end of my nose with a finger. "Hey, don't play shrink with me. I'm a big girl; my parents are grown-ups. We'll work it out. You just keep your head down and smile at them the next time you see them."

"And don't talk shop."

"And don't talk shop."

I'd learned quickly the first time I met her parents that they thought their daughter being in theater was demeaning. They also thought her career aspirations were a waste of good money. And they particularly were not impressed by what I did. Computers, her father once said to me, bored him.

"This is going to be quite an adventure," she added on her way out the door.

My cat meowed from his perch on top of the largest and warmest computer monitor. Even he thought it was going to be an adventure. I couldn't say that I disagreed with either one of them.

I was just getting to the papers from the school. Yesterday, I'd worked hard to catch up at the office and had finally freed some time for this morning. I had a stack of reference checks sitting on my desk to do for an electronics firm that was expanding in Beaverton and two names from the Navy recruiter to check to see if the recruiters were telling the truth on their enlistment papers. That didn't give me a lot of time to go through this information.

I'd learned long ago that most political bodies work in code, meaning that what you see on the surface usually represents something else beneath the surface. A high school had layers of politics built into it. You had staff dealing with staff, staff dealing with administration, students dealing with staff, students dealing with administration, and students dealing with students. Power or politics permeated them all.

I found it interesting that the yearbook, representing last year's group, had a lively theme of celebration, complete with bubbly bottles of drink spread throughout the book. A careful look at the labels on the bottles showed the words "School

Spirit" written in. That all sounded pretty harmless until you saw the first issue of the newspaper for the year with several letters to the editor from parents complaining that the bottles in the yearbook were suggestive of drinking alcohol, totally inappropriate for a school annual. An article in the second issue of the newspaper announced that last year's yearbook advisor had been replaced with a new one for this year.

The yearbook also showed a picture of a principal who appeared to be fun-loving and liked by students if the photos were any indication. He was often seen in pictures in the book participating in events such as pie-eating contests, kidding around with kids in the halls, or looking relaxed and informal in meetings with staff and students.

The article in the paper announcing the new principal suggested that the fun-loving principal would have more fun in the district office where he had been transferred to work on an alternative education program. He was quoted as saying that he was sorry to be leaving, but the district office thought it best.

A second article in the same issue listed new rules being instituted by the new administration. From the gist of the rules, I learned that this year it was going to be harder to skip classes, to leave school, to participate in activities without good enough grades, and to vandalize without harsh punishment. Apparently the old principal had not run a tight enough ship, and the new principal was expected to fix that. From what I saw, she at least had everyone uptight.

Several articles and two editorials referred to a problem with gang graffiti on school grounds. One of the articles announced that two youths had been caught and punished for vandalizing a restroom. One editorial obliquely suggested that discipline too harsh sometimes got the opposite results, that instead of tempering a behavior it only inflamed it. The next issue of the newspaper announced that a new advisor had been assigned to the publications staff.

Ms. Cray's memos to the staff were blunt, critical, and threatening. She blamed many of the ills at the school on poor staff supervision of students. She didn't want students sent out of the classroom for any reason, she wanted the staff in the hallways during passing times, she set up a schedule of staff supervision before and after school, and she planned to include in evaluations whether or not the staff contributed to an improved atmosphere at the school.

From the information she gave me, I found it difficult to know what the students or staff felt about all this. Once the advisor of the newspaper was replaced, no more critical letters or editorials appeared. A clue, though, came from one of the reports that she had submitted to the staff. Expulsions, suspensions, and detentions were up dramatically. She seemed to be proud of that fact. As she said in one memo, she would not tolerate disobedience from anyone, implying staff as well. Students apparently did have hard feelings about the changes, but they either didn't have a channel to express them, or they were rushed out the door if they did.

In her report on the shooting, Ms. Cray stated quite clearly that she felt it was only a matter of time before something terrible and violent happened to the two youths who were shot. They had been caught writing gang graffiti on the walls of a restroom. They were failing their classes. They often skipped classes and left campus. They were known to be heavily involved in gang activity outside of school. Although many people wanted to make a connection with the school and the shootings, she did not think the two were related. Yes, the boys were in the act of painting graffiti on the walls of the school when they were shot, and yes this seemed to be an act of revenge because she had suspended them that day, but she was convinced from her investigation that the shootings were gang-related and the result of something that had happened off campus. She did not give any reasons why she thought this was true or any evidence to suggest it was.

My guess is that the superintendent wanted a report he could wave in front of the school board declaring the school an innocent bystander, and the board wanted a report that they could wave in the face of parents, saying that the shootings had nothing to do with the school.

This is why people pay me so much money. Finding the truth can be a real challenge, especially when dealing with political groups who are so adept at burying it.

If I chose to pursue it some more, I would probably discover that everyone was a bit sensitive because the heat was on at the high school. If the kids weren't happy, their parents probably weren't very happy, either. If the teachers weren't happy, you can bet the union wasn't very happy as well. My guess was that Ms. Cray had turned up the heat too high on the pressure cooker and now she was working really hard not to be blown away when it exploded. The shootings were certainly something that could get an unloved administrator blown away in a political environment.

What did all of this have to do with the shootings? Diane was right. There had to be a reason for them starting at the high school. The second and third shootings could be traced back to news reports. So could the first. The school newspaper had announced that two students had been caught vandalizing. Knowing what it was like when I was in high school, my guess is everyone in the building knew who they were. One staff memo referred to the two by name. Did that mean the killer came from the school? I'd have like to think so, but an article in the newspaper pointed out with pride that not only was every student getting a paper this year, but every parent would have one mailed to the house. If that wasn't enough to make my job really difficult, the article went on to say that stacks of newspapers would be left with each of the fifty advertisers in it so the businesses could hand them out to customers. Exponentially, I was back to everyone in the city being a possible suspect.

Diane returned from her car with the clothes on hangers. "How's it going?" she asked as she walked by.

"I'll need to go over the information a few more times, but for now I can say for sure that the shooter is one of maybe a hundred thousand who had a chance to read one of these school newspapers."

She glanced at the papers. "Your number's too high," she said. "Few students read the whole school newspaper—they only read about the things they were in. Teachers pretty much ignore it unless the stories have something to do with them. Parents usually only read about their kids. Strangers might take one of the papers, but unless they have a connection to the school, they won't read it. Your shooter might be one of five hundred, at worst." She disappeared into the apartment.

I had to admire her optimism, and her good sense. She was right. If I could find a way to narrow the number down to 500, I could start cross checking with other information such as hunting licenses, etc. But first I had to find a way to reduce the number.

Diane popped back in the room. "Dress rehearsal tonight is at seven, right?"

"Right."

"I won't be there much before then. I've reserved a U-Haul truck for ten on Saturday morning at that Texaco near my place. Do you think you could pick it up for me?"

"Sure. You wouldn't want to go out for breakfast first and then the two of us could pick it up?"

"I'll need all the time I can get to pack."

"That's fine, then. I'll see you tonight."

She kissed me before she left, something she almost never did. I was going to have a lot of new things to get used to. I can't even remember what it was like to be married to my first wife before the kids came along. This was going to be like that, however it was.

I smiled. Although I didn't remember much about that time, I certainly didn't remember anything bad about it. Diane and I might just have one hell of a good time. And then, of course, I immediately felt guilty about being so optimistic.

I spent most of the day scanning the files that Whitlock had given me; I couldn't find the virus.

In my business, the worst fear is that I'll run up against someone who's more clever than I am. Given an equal playing field, dumb luck might still swing things my way, but computers were not an equal playing field. Anytime numbers are concerned, the possibilities are endless. A brilliant man might just find a way to outsmart everyone using numbers. I just didn't want to be the victim.

I sat back in my chair, stared at the computer screen and reviewed what I knew: An e-mail message said the files could and would be destroyed if $50,000 wasn't paid immediately. And, when the money wasn't paid, files *were* destroyed. Only a hidden program, which is what a virus is, could carry out the threat.

But writing to a computer hard drive is not like writing on paper with invisible ink. A record of a program exists. Finding it is the only trick. In this case, we know the program would not be stored with some obvious name like "virus." The blackmailer would want to hide it as carefully as he could, which means he or she would have worked hard to disguise it as something else, attaching it to an account order.

Even then I should be able to find it. I opened each account and searched for anything that looked out of order. Next I estimated the amount of space an account should take up on the hard drive and compared it to the amount that was actually taken up. If nothing else, this should have led me to the account with the overweight megabytes.

Only, there wasn't one. Nor could I find any hidden files in any of the programming. Basically, because this was a business machine with a special use, I didn't find the kinds of things you find on a home computer, such as games and temp. files and old, out-dated programs. Everything on the tape suggested the computer was used for one thing, and that was all that showed up there, with no extra baggage to account for a virus.

This added up to several possibilities. One was that I didn't have all the information on this backup tape. The only way I would be able to tell is if I sat down on the computer myself and compared the two.

The second possibility was extremely remote. Instead of being stored on the hard drive as RAM, the virus was stored on the ROM. The idea was staggering. Not only would the person have to have the equipment and skill to put a virus onto permanent memory, but he'd have to get into the computer to switch the doctored ROM with the original. I didn't entirely discount the idea, but I wouldn't pursue it unless everything else failed.

The third possibility was that the virus was being run remotely. Somehow the blackmailer was able to send the program by modem to do its duty. That meant the virus should show up on the next backup tape I got. Maybe. The virus could be sent to wipe out files, and then be programmed to eliminate all traces of itself after it was done. I could do a quick fix if this was the case. I could write a short program that would screen out anything that didn't fall in the perimeters of a typical order, sending back a message that any order outside of these perimeters would have to be sent by mail or fax.

If the blackmailer was really clever, he'd have the virus back in a short time wrapped in a cloak that looked just like a typical clothing order.

The last possibility meant this fellow was *truly* clever, and that he had created a "stealth" virus that simply wouldn't show up under a normal investigation. That idea caused my heart to race a bit, but not to stop. Just like invisible ink held over a flame, an invisible file would come up, too, with the right technique. I'd just have to find out what that technique was.

I finished my day trying to locate Mark Whitlock. I went to the obvious first: I called his lawyer. I told him who I was and what I was suppose to be doing. He had a good laugh and said he wouldn't tell me where Mark was, even if he knew.

"Okay," I said, "How about if I say I'm from Publishers Clearing House and I have a million dollar check for Mr. Whitlock?"

The lawyer laughed again. "He wouldn't take it, because he wouldn't give Margorie another chance to take a penny from him. Mark's gone. He means to stay gone."

"Why are you so sure?"

Because I'm his best friend and his lawyer, and he hasn't even told me where he is."

That parting shot almost got me on the phone with Mrs. Whitlock to tell her not to waste her money and my time. But I didn't. Lawyers protected their clients. Friends lied for friends. Although I tended to believe the lawyer, I wanted conformation from other sources that Mark was indeed "disappeared" before I gave up.

THIRTEEN

He paused at the head of the alley, looked both ways to make sure no one was in sight, and then stepped into the darkness. The bakery was the first business on this block that he would hit. He planned to do a thorough job of spray painting graffiti on the walls, as well as cracking a few windows. He didn't want to do too much damage, because he didn't want to have to work too hard tomorrow.

Tomorrow he would offer his services to the baker to clean up the mess; he would even settle for minimum wage. The next day one of his friends would stop by and suggest to the baker that this sort of damage could be avoided if the store owner would pay for a little security. If the owner said no, they'd be back in time, once everyone let down their guard. Next time a different buddy would offer to repair the damages. Somebody new would be around to discuss insurance.

This scam had worked well in a variety of cities. So far it was off to a slow start in Portland. These people still believed the police could protect them from scams like this. They might be slow to learn, but in the end they would learn. Short of parking a squad car in front of the bakery every night, the cops couldn't stop them. In time they'd have lots of money rolling in, from the baker, from the bookstore, from the café ...

He used a black enamel spray paint. It dried fast and was hell to get off. He began with the usual. "Kill niggers and Jews!" That always fooled them because he was black. When his buddy did it, he sprayed, "Kill the spics." He, of course, was a Latino. This scam was fool-proof.

He had just bent down to finish a line when his whole face started to burn. Instinctively he dropped the can and rolled back into the shadows of the alley. He wiped his hand across his face. His fingers were covered with grit. "What the hell?" And then he knew what the hell. Slightly above where his head had been just a few seconds ago was a small crater in the bricks. Someone had taken a shot at him. He used his feet to shove himself against the opposite wall. The street was dimly lighted, but bright enough for him to see that no one was there. The shot had to have come from the other way, off to his right.

He had cased the alley earlier in the day. He could get out the other end, or he could get up on the garbage dumpster to the fire escape and make it to the roofs. As long as the guy stayed where he was.

The blast so surprised him that he slammed his head against the alley wall. For a moment he sat, dazed, his ears ringing. He touched a hand to his face. The fingers came away wet and sticky. He was bleeding. His whole head was bleeding.

He started laughing as soon as he understood the smell. The blast had been the spray can exploding. Something had literally ripped it to shreds. The paint had covered the front of his shirt, too. He touched the liquid and brought it to his nose.

Fear flashed through him. He reached down again and ran his fingers along the ragged edge of his shirt. Something, probably part of the spray can, had slashed across his stomach. Blood was pooling in his lap.

He had to do something. Too much blood was coming out.

He couldn't make it out the other end of alley. If he stayed where he was, he'd bleed to death. He'd probably bleed to death anyway, but he had to get in the light so someone could see him, but getting into the light meant getting shot at again.

He touched his stomach. His hand was slick with blood. He knew what he had to do. He crawled toward the head of the alley. As he pulled himself into the light, he waited. He knew it would happen so fast that his lights would simply go out.

A minute passed and he was still alive. Several people stood across the street, staring at him. Nobody came over to help. Maybe they were the ones who did it, he thought. And then he heard the approach of the siren.

FOURTEEN

Buck, who considered it manly to sleep on the opposite corner of the bed from my head, now burrows his way under the covers at night and sleeps on his back in Diane's armpit.

He defers to her on all issues, especially concerning food, and he only tolerates attention from me. I should have made him sign a loyalty oath before I took him in. Now, after all these years, I find that he actually prefers the female of my species to me. I would make a big deal out of my feelings of rejection, but Diane would want to analyze the relationship between Buck and me for deeper meaning. I don't want to believe there is any deeper meaning.

None of us has been in a hurry to get up, including Buck. The last two nights the show sold out, and the matinée, our final performance, is expected to be a sellout, too. Our group has a good following and good support, but the combination of a comedy and Diane seem to get our biggest crowds.

We'd be tempted to use Diane all the time, but wisely she refuses. She doesn't want to wear out her welcome with an audience. Of the six performances a year, she will star in two. In two she will take smaller parts, against type preferably, for the challenge. She then sits out two.

I sit out two a year, as well. Burnout is the biggest reason amateur theater groups fail. Too few people try to do too much of the work. I'll sit out the next play, do tech work on the one after that, and then direct. I'm sure that after I've directed a play, I'll want to sit out the one after to recover. I haven't seen a director yet who doesn't have a faraway look once the show is about to close.

After the matinée, we'll meet at Jake's for a cast party. Unlike most theater groups, we don't strike the set after the last performance. We wait until the next play is planned and the set designed. To save money, we reuse everything we can. Often we go in and shift around a few flats to create the next set without pulling a whole lot of it down.

Diane mumbled at me from under the covers.

"What?"

A hand came out and pawed away the blankets from her face. "Just because I'm living here doesn't mean we have to have sex every night."

These are the types of statements that really confuse a male. Last night she gave no indication that she didn't want to make love. In fact, I was the one who seemed to be about a step behind. I tried to set just the right tone of voice so she wouldn't think I was being overly sensitive. "We don't have to make love tonight."

Her hand waved feebly in the air. "No, no. I want to make love tonight. Sunday night lovemaking makes me start out Monday with a clear head."

When it comes to lovemaking, I'm pretty easy to please. "We'll skip the next night, then."

The hand waved feebly again. "No good. We'll want to celebrate my first day in the office."

"The night after?"

The hand waved. "I'll tell you when."

I helped her unbury her face from the covers. Buck opened one eye, stared menacingly at me, and then shut it. "Hi," I said, kissing her on the lips.

"No, no, no," she said. "Morning breath."

"Is it that bad?"

"Not you, me."

"How about breakfast in bed? I'll bring us some breath mints while I'm at it."

"Bring Buck something, too."

The cat opened both of his eyes, looked at me, and smiled. I swear he smiled. "Sometime in the near future we will have to talk about Buck."

She yawned and then groped at the covers to bury her head again, saying, "Ooooh, do I hear jealousy in your voice or what? Buck's just a cat."

"Who's died and gone to cat heaven."

She mumbled something in response.

I lowered the tray down to counter height below and tied it off. I'd put an eye in the ceiling and rigged a small rope through it. The end was attached to the tray something like a cargo net. This allowed me to run things up to the loft without having to carry them up the ladder.

I was in the kitchen, setting up Diane's Mrs. Tea next to my Mr. Coffee when the phone rang. The phone in the apartment was on a separate line and had a private number. I didn't give out the number to many people and had asked that Diane do the same.

"Dad?"

Oh, yes. The children. They were rarely out of my mind, but I kept them in a safe little niche at the back of my brain. To bring them to the forefront often meant more anger than I could cope with.

"Dad? Dad? It's been so long since anyone has called me that, I hardly recognize the name." I propped the phone under my chin and continued to make the tea. This was eldest child, Cindi, who liked neither her first name or her last name. I tried to guess what she wanted. I hadn't forgotten her birthday. She wasn't old enough to want a car. Hopefully she didn't need a prom dress, although she was getting to that age that all father's, distant or otherwise, fear. She would be dating soon.

"Ben and I want you to send us some money to get mom a Mother's Day present."

Wonderful things flashed through my head, like the incredibly amount of money I send to their mother each month, and the generous amount I included for their allowances. To mention any of this was to open myself up to heaps of abuse.

"How much?"

"Fifty."

My former wife was like a gift that keeps getting instead of giving. I fight off the sense of resentment I feel when I realize just how little I get from this flood of money I send them. I try to tell myself that it's the price I must pay to be free of Sarah, but that usually leads me into depression. I am buying myself out of something I reluctantly had to end. Sarah was the one who refused to commit to the marriage.

"I feel lucky to get off with fifty dollars."

"Each?"

"Don't push your luck. No mother alive is worth a hundred dollars."

"Dad!"

"Let me get this right. Does this mean you are talking to me again?"

"At least for today."

"What about your brother?"

"He wants to talk to you, too."

I looked out the window for the flash of light or the rainbow, or some other glorious symbol that would explain the mystery of my children.

"How's life?"

"I wrote you a long letter telling you all about it. It's kind of boring. I'm still working on breasts and I haven't got my braces off yet."

"Hmmm," I said, not sure that any comment I could make would be adequate. "My mother had breasts. Your mother has breasts. I'm sure, dear, you will do as well. It's in the genes."

She sighed. "Thanks Dad, that helped."

I wiped the imaginary sweat from my brow, and, with a flick of the wrist, sent it flying off in space. I had handled that remarkably well.

"Does that mean I'm going to be as short as you?"

Ah, Ben was listening in on the other line. "I'm six feet tall, Ben. I can't promise that you'll be six feet, but I'm sure you won't stay five two forever."

"Geez, dad, if you're not six ten, you're nobody in this world."

"That's only a height requirement for staying in Southern California. You're allowed to be shorter in other states."

"Gawd!"

We talked for another ten minutes. They tried to convince me how small their lives were, and I tried to convince them that they were on a path to gianthood. More than anything what they seemed to need from me was a reassurance that I loved them and that they would do wonders with their lives. Our rather nasty divorce punched holes in both of those notions for them.

In the end, as I knew she would, Sarah came on the phone. "Your children need to see you," she said.

"It's nice to see that refusing to talk to me for six months has made their hearts grow fonder."

As always she brushed aside any criticism from me. It only took up time when she could be criticizing me. "I think you should come down and visit them when school is out for a week or two."

"You were always very good as scheduling my time."

"They need time with their father."

"Have them come up here."

"Really? So they can do what? Live in tiny, cramped quarters and watch you work?"

"I'll let them feed the cat this time."

"Tom, you're impossible. You've got the absentee father part down pat. You send the support payments on time, you pay their medical and dental bills, and you never let a birthday or holiday go by unnoticed. Don't you think it's time you threw into that some of yourself?"

"Divorce is hell."

"Don't do that. Divorce is divorce. That's the way it is. I made mistakes. You made mistakes. We're beyond fixing that. But the children still belong to both of us."

"Not according to the custody agreement."

"I agree the custody agreement is unfair, but I was protecting the kids from you. You either lavish too much attention on them, or not enough. You don't have a clue how to be a parent on a daily basis."

"It would have been nice to be given the opportunity to learn."

"You had the kids during the summer. They got tired of your inept parenting."

"Look, we could probably argue this forever, which is okay, because it's on your phone bill, but I'm not sure we can work out a resolution."

"I'll reverse the charges. Will that help?"

I had to laugh. I couldn't help it. She was always able to make me laugh even when I was down in the dumps. "No, don't. But I'll see what I can do about visiting them this summer. I'm not involved in the next theater production, and I should be able to clear the workload for at least a long weekend."

"Clear it for a week."

"Sure, as long as you don't mind not getting one of those checks."

"Have you taken a look at your stocks lately?"

Whoops. She wasn't suppose to know about those. "What stocks?"

"The ones I let you keep out of the kindness of my heart. You got in at seven dollars a share. They're now going for one hundred thirty-four a share."

"Okay, so I won't miss a payment." I was given 5,000 shares in the company as part of my severance package. I still had the shares. Even after capital gains taxes, I'd have a tough time convincing anyone I couldn't take a week off work.

"I'll let you know when I'm coming down."

"I'll tell the children to look forward to it."

I pushed the button to turn off the phone and then returned it to its base. I had managed to get most of breakfast ready while on the phone. Bagels and cream cheese, toast and jam, tea, coffee, and orange juice.

When I stepped out from under the loft and looked up, I saw Diane with her chin on her hands on the railing. "I think you're going to be my first client," she said.

"If it's prostitution you're talking about, you can have everything I own."

"You know what I'm talking about. You need to spend more time with your kids, especially now, at their ages."

I transferred the food to the tray. "You know they don't want to spend time up here."

"Then you need to spend more time in California."

I finished putting the food on the tray. She began to pull it up. "At the expense of my business?" I asked.

"Oregon's Electronic Forest. California's Silicon Valley. An enterprising man could find a way to work both groups for the benefit of everyone."

I didn't want to admit it, but the thought had crossed my mind already. These groups often worked in isolation from each other. That was natural because they often competed. On the other hand, most of the companies had lots of areas in which they did not compete. A good liaison person with a knowledge of the industry might well be able to sell services showing the companies how they could help each other in the areas where they did not compete.

"Don't bug me," I said. "I'm working on this father thing."

"I know. I heard. Your mother had breasts and so does your ex wife."

"Hey, some of this is new to me."

"That's why you might need some help."

She had the tray sitting on the bed. I climbed in beside her. "Would I have to pay?"

"Of course."

"Would I get a discount?"

"No way."

"You're tough."

"I'm going to need every penny I can get. By the way, you didn't bring up anything for Buck."

"The piece of toast with butter and no jam is for Buck."

"Toast?"

"Just the way he likes it." To illustrate the point, Buck

cautiously approached the tray, grabbed his piece of toast by the corner, and dragged it off the bed.

"That's funny," she said. "He looks to me like a cat who would like jam."

For the rest of the morning, until it was time to go to the theater, we each took care of our own business. I cleaned the apartment and dusted and straightened up the office. Diane went up to her own office to organize her things and get ready for clients, she hoped.

She would have to wait several months before she could get an ad in the yellow pages. For now she had to settle for her name as part of an information hotline for counselors, and for referrals from others, such as doctors, lawyers, and ministers. She had taken a lot time over the last few months, as she was finishing up school, to go around the community to other professionals who dealt with family problems and introduce herself. She didn't know how much business would come from it, but without a listing in the phone book, she had to do something.

She would spend much of this week on the phone letting people know her office was now open, and she planned an open house for acquaintances and family friends in the near future. Right now the only thing she could do was to spread the word as far and as often as she could.

While Diane was at her office, I lectured Buck about his two-faced nature. I seemed to have reached him, because he slinked out the window and disappeared. Later he came back and left a dead pigeon on my recliner, a sure sign of undying devotion.

FIFTEEN

We returned from Jake's just a little bit tipsy. The celebration was a happy one. The play had closed to a packed house. Between ticket sales and contributions, we have pulled in over $25,000. We drank to being able to pay the rent. We drank to fact the electricity wouldn't be turned off. We drank to the next play that now had the money to get it going.

When I was unlocked the office door, I was greeted to a melodious, "You have a phone message."

Diane giggled. "Should I ever fail at acting, I want to have my voice digitized so I can have it spread nationwide on every computer ever made."

I shut the door and made sure it was locked. "Such low ambition," I said. "Besides, Doris has the market cornered." Doris was the digitized voice in my 24-hour computer. She announced when I had e-mail or voice messages. The computer had a sleep mode that kept it quiet unless something came through its modem, then it would handle the task and shut itself down again. I had it rigged so that when I turned on the office light, the computer would automatically come to life and tell me if any messages had come in while I was out.

"Why don't you just turn off the voice on that thing and

have it peep or flash the screen or something when you have a message?"

"Fire my secretary? And you were accusing me of jealousy."

"Doesn't the voice irritate you?"

I clicked the mouse button a couple of times until I got to the voice mail for me. "Not really," I said. "On some days, Doris is the only voice I hear."

I hadn't meant that to sound sad or tragic, but by the way Diane looked at me, it must have sounded one or the other. I thought she was going to cry.

The computer replayed the message: "Mr. Walkinshaw, my name is Beth Armstrong. I'm the former newspaper advisor at Fremont High. I'd like to talk to you about the shootings. You can reach me at home." She left the phone number.

"My," Diane said, "I wonder what she has to say?"

"Let's find out." I used the speaker phone on the desk to dial out.

She answered on the third ring. "Beth Armstrong."

"This is Tom Walkinshaw, Ms. ..."

"Mrs."

"Mrs. Armstrong. I'm returning your call." I switched on the speaker so Diane could hear.

"You're not related to that racing fellow in England, Tom Walkinshaw, are you?"

I laughed. "No, I'm not. I do get asked occasionally, though. I sometimes wonder if anyone has ever asked him if he is related to me."

"Forgive me. I was curious when I first heard your name. But that's not why I called."

I sat on the corner of the desk. Diane picked up a note pad and pencil from the desk and started taking notes. "You mentioned the shootings."

"Tragic," she said. "I knew both of the boys. They weren't as bad as many people made them out to be, at least in the right environment. Sometimes it's a shame we have to send them home at night."

"I imagine that the tally of both successes and failures would get to a teacher after a time."

"That's quite observant. You do decry the failures. And you do lose a pound of flesh each time you find a former student you could barely tolerate who now makes four times the amount of money you do."

"I'll keep my profession, thank you."

"And your profession is a fascinating one. I've tried to steer my journalism students to other careers besides working on a newspaper. What you do certainly could be done by a journalist."

I didn't know if I should be pleased with that assessment or not. I had started out in engineering and ended up in computers. "What can you tell me about the shootings?"

"Not much in the way of clues, I'm afraid. I just wanted you to know that I asked my former staff members to poke around and see what they could find out about the killings. Several of them are actually quite good, and we all know that buried in the student body is the answer to every secret."

"And what did they find out?"

"Very little. We stayed after school one day and kicked around what we knew and what we'd learned. This wasn't something done by one of our students. It wasn't something done related to gangs."

"You're sure of that?"

"As positive as I can be. That doesn't mean our school doesn't harbor a psychopath, but if we do, he's very secretive. I've never heard of any crime being committed by one of our students that wasn't known about by one or more other students."

"Is there anyone on the staff who makes you nervous?"

She laughed. "Only the principal."

"I figured out that the two of you must have had a disagreement."

"I can't say much about it," she said, "because I have initiated a grievance against her, and several of my journalism students are planning a lawsuit. Most administrators have trouble with freedom of the press when it comes to students, but most live with it. In her ignorance, my principal has stepped over all the lines that might have protected her."

"So, besides being a little power intensive, do you think she's a psychopath, too?"

"No, not at all."

"Any others who might be?"

"The football coach talks a lot about destroying opponents; a PE teacher is a hard-core feminist; a math teacher supports any cause as long as it's liberal; and a science teacher prefers to teach Creationism over Darwinism. Those are pretty much our extremists. I couldn't imagine any of them intentionally hurting a fly, let alone killing a person."

"Is there anything you want to add?"

"No, that's it. After last night's shooting, I felt like I needed to share my feelings with you."

Diane and I both shared a surprised look. "Last night's shooting?"

"Yes. The one in Northeast Portland. I'm surprised you haven't heard about it."

"I'm in a theater group and we wrapped up a production today. I haven't had a chance to read the paper or see the news."

"The police have say it was the same person."

"Thank you for calling. Would you mind if I gave you a call if I have any questions about the school, staff, or students?"

"Not at all, but you'd better call me at home."

"I wouldn't want you to waste your school time with calls from me. Goodnight."

Diane headed for the apartment, saying, "I'll see if I can find anything on the news."

"I'll go downstairs and get the paper out of my box."

A half an hour later we knew pretty much what everyone knew about the shooting. The victim had not been shot, but injured from the exploding paint can. He was in serious condition, but expected to recover. He had not seen his assailant.

We were stretched out on the bed surrounded by the parts of the newspaper. Diane was reading the comics while I thought about these new developments.

"He missed," I said.

"Apparently not by much."

"A miss is a miss."

She lowered the comics. "Why does that fascinate you?"

"I read the autopsy reports on the others. He didn't wing them. He literally blew their heads off with a single shot. All hits, dead center. Now we have one that was slightly high and to the right."

She smiled a patient smile. "He missed."

"He had to miss for a reason."

"Maybe he wanted to miss."

"And he really doesn't mean to harm these people and he really wants to get caught."

"Okay, okay. Why do you think he missed?"

"I'm guessing he got hurried. Somebody might have come along, or he might have just happened on the tagger and wasn't ready for a good shoot."

Buck crawled on top of the comics in Diane's lap and curled up on them. "Buck, baby," she said, "don't make me chose between you and the comics." He looked up at her with adoring eyes and the comics lost out. "And?"

"And, I don't know what that means. Taggers may be hard to come by right now, and he's having to go out and prowl for them. If that's the case, he'll be spotted eventually if he hasn't been already. I wonder what he'll do if his source of taggers dries up?"

"You really are good at this," she said. "You think of the strangest things."

"So what will he do?"

"How many dead taggers does it take to quench a man's thirst for dead taggers? Serial killers have been known to stop."

"And if he isn't the kind to stop?"

"He'll find someone else who pisses him off to shoot."

"We might learn a lot from something like that."

She shook her head in disgust. "You want him to start shooting other people so you can learn more about what makes him tick?"

"Only if he just nicks them. Not kill, just nicks."

"Why don't you just find the bugger and make everyone happy. And take your cat. He's not allowed to come between me and my comics."

I climbed off the bed. "I'm going to go down and enter this latest information into the computer."

I was halfway down the ladder when she said, "You forgot the cat."

"There's another sheet of comics in the paper. Read those and then offer to trade him. Buck is a reasonable guy. He's open to negotiations."

When I flicked on the lights of the office, Doris said, "You have e-mail."

I wasn't surprised. I often got e-mail on a Sunday night, usually about some project I was working on the next day. I clicked on my server and downloaded the message.

I stared at the message for a long time. Lots of things ran through my head. The fact that it didn't have a return address was one of them. I tried some hotshot computer tricks to see if I could trace the message. I ended up at the Multnomah County Library. I was sure the message hadn't originated from there. The library was on-line. Anyone with a little computer knowledge could channel a message through the library, making it impossible to trace.

I hadn't thought I would trace it. People who thought their e-mail could be traced didn't leave messages like this. I read it one more time: Data-dumb, data-dumb, Data-man, data-dead.

I shut down the computer and turned out the lights in the office. When I climbed back up to the loft, I found both Diane and Buck asleep. Buck somehow had managed to sprawl himself on top of both sets of comics. I turned out the lights and slipped under the covers, but it was a long time before I fell asleep.

SIXTEEN

I got up early the next morning, which was easy to do because I hadn't slept much. Diane was up before me and out of the shower just as I went in. She was excited about her first day of work, and I was anxious to clear my desk so I could free up a couple of hours this morning.

After the shower, I poured myself a cup of coffee, (freshly brewed by Diane) and set it next to her freshly brewed tea. Already this felt comfortable. I had to remove Buck from my chair at the table. He wasn't happy about it. I got the feeling he was the one who was jealous of me when it came to Diane.

She sat at the table with her hands wrapped around her cup and her eyes searching my face over its rim. "I think this is going to be okay," she said.

"I do, too."

She finished her tea and then rushed out the door with a quick kiss and an even faster goodbye. I was happy for her enthusiasm. I hoped it lasted. It had for me, this time around. I hadn't felt any of the discontent for this job that I had at Hewlett Packard or in California. I was my own boss and I liked it. Diane would be her own boss, and I suspect she will like that, too.

I had the two reports completed and in the mail by ten

o'clock. That meant I needed to be back by one to meet with a new client. Three hours, I hoped, would be enough time.

I usually rode public transportation around the city, either the bus or the MAX rail line. I was all for conserving natural resources and maximizing mass transit. Except on a day when I was in a hurry. I walked the two blocks to the office building where my car was kept.

I stopped in front of a large, cast-iron gate that covered an entrance that led to the basement of the building. I used a key to open a smaller gate the size of a door set into the larger gate. A few minutes later I was back in my 1968 Austin Healey 3000, restored to original condition, including the ice-blue-over-white two-tone paint job. I used a remote to open the gate, and then close it once I was through.

The day was clear, sunny but crisp. I didn't care how cool it was. When the sun was out, that was reason to put the top down on the car. I liked to smell the city while I drove through it, gas fumes and all.

First I drove to the neighborhood where the last shooting had occurred. From the newspaper account, it was easy to pick out the details of the shooting. The street, lined with small businesses in a basically poor neighborhood, was busy. As I walked around and looked, no one paid any attention to me. They probably thought I was just another reporter.

My next stop was to see Lieutenant Wilson. I finally tracked him down at a community police office near where the shooting took place, one of those remote locations spread around high crime areas in the city. The idea was to make the police more accessible to residents in the poor parts of the town.

The sergeant in the front office directed me to a small room in the back when I asked for Wilson. I found him sitting at a desk reading through a pile of weekend crime reports. He didn't seemed surprised to see me when he finally noticed I was standing in the doorway.

"Walkinshaw. I had a feeling I'd see you today."

I raised an eyebrow. "Any reason?"

"Another shooting. I figured you'd have to do some scrambling around to earn those big bucks you're being paid."

"I'm surprised you're not out doing some investigating. It's still your case, isn't it?"

"You're wrong and you're right. I am investigating, and the case is still mine."

"Finding anything?"

"I'll know when I see it."

He left it hanging at that, but I wasn't bad at reading upside down, so I could see the notes he was making on the crime reports. He was going through all the reports to see if anything suspicious may have happened in the neighborhood that might relate to the shooting. He also had a handful of traffic citations next to the reports. He was being thorough, a sign of a good cop.

"I just took a look at the crime scene," I said.

"And?"

"I'm guessing the shooter parked down a side street. Since your victim didn't say, at least in the newspaper reports, that he had seen anything suspicious, I'm guessing the shooter was already parked when the tagger came along."

He interrupted me. "So he just happens to be parked there, in a section of town that's not too safe in daylight let alone late at night."

"There's quite a bit of graffiti on that business street. I think the shooter was parked there because it was a good place to get a shot at another tagger."

"Interesting," he said. "The shooter's now out cruising for crimes of opportunity instead of letting them come to him."

"Bad press," I said. "Taggers are suddenly scarce."

"And then what happened?"

"His victim came along. From the first it was all wrong. The shooter was parked in a place that only allowed him to see part of the street. When the tagger ducked in the alley, he couldn't see him at all. In that brief moment when the tagger's head appeared out of the shadows, he hurried a shot. He might have still had a hit, but your tagger ducked back down to dot the i on 'nigger.' The shooter will probably go after people with good hand writing next."

"So why'd he shoot the paint can?"

"Anger. The tagger rolled back into the alley out of sight. As far as the shooter knew, he was long gone down the alley. He took it out on the spray can. He was probably pretty surprised when it exploded and made such a loud noise, loud enough to bring people in the neighborhood outside to see what it was."

"And what happened then?"

"He left. If it weren't for the noise, he might have tried stalking the tagger, but now he had to leave before he was seen."

"Why wasn't he seen?"

"I don't know," I said. "You tell me. I was kind of hoping he was."

"Good news and bad news. The good news is he was seen. The bad news is he was parked on a dark street in a dark vehicle, and he drove off with the lights out. Folks heard it. They saw something moving. But, not one of them could say what it was."

"That makes our man very, very lucky."

"There's not much worse than a psychopath who can shoot straight and is lucky."

"Did I get anything wrong?" I asked.

Wilson tapped his pencil on his note pad. Finally he said, "You know as much as we do. That means you're as right or wrong as we are."

I wasn't sure if that was a compliment or not. "One more thing."

He groaned. I was expecting some kind of lecture on how busy he was, but instead he said, "What?"

"The killer is somehow linked to Fremont High."

"I thought you rejected that idea at one time."

"I had, until I started wondering why the shootings started there. Nothing about it said it was random. The shooter had to know the boys would be there that night, or they would be there on some night at that time. He had to be waiting for them. That brings it back to someone who has something to do with Fremont."

"Great—that narrows it down to a few thousand people. They'll probably want to draft you as chief of detectives with that kind of investigative work."

I handed him a sheet of paper with my e-mail message. "That came across my computer last night."

"What, are you trying to suggest that you are somehow blessed and the shooter is now communicating with you?"

"It showed up after I went out to Fremont. The staff and students knew I was there. I think it's a message to try to warn me off this case."

He looked disgusted. "The cops don't scare him, but some computer weenie does. Is your life that boring and your imagination that good you have to manufacture such notions?"

"That's a threatening message," I said.

"Congratulations. I get them all the time. Notes left on my windshield. Voice mail at work. Letters that come to my home. My advice to you is carry a big gun and keep looking over your shoulder."

"You don't think it's from him?"

"How many deadbeat dads have you tracked down?"

"A lot."

"And you think they don't have a Hate Tom Walkinshaw Club?"

"I've never thought about it. This is my first threatening note."

"Stay in your business and it won't be your last. One of those deadbeat dads you catch, or one of those tax cheaters, or one of those felons you discover in a reference check will want you to know they're not happy with your services. It looks like one of them already has."

He might have been right, but my gut didn't think so. "Would you do me a favor?"

"What?"

"If you're wrong and this guy wastes me, would you take care of my cat?"

He looked through the open doorway to my car beyond. "Is that your Healey?"

"Yeah."

"I'll take care of it, too."

"You're all heart, lieutenant."

As I turned to leave, he said, "Thanks for the report. You can go give it to Curry now. Just make sure if you're still alive to make another one, that I get it first."

I was steaming by the time I reached my car. I hadn't intended this to be a report to him. I hadn't gone to Curry first because—well, face it, Curry is a computer nerd, not a cop. If someone threatens you, you want a cop like Wilson looking into it, not one like Curry.

As I drove away, I had to smile to myself. That was probably the same thing Wilson was thinking. The force should have gone to him and not to me to solve this crime. When they brought me in it was like a slap in the face.

It was lunch time by the time I had the car safely stowed away. Diane and I hadn't talked about lunch, so I decided I'd stick with my normal routine. I walked a couple of blocks up to corner bar/cafe that served the best hamburgers in the city. During the week, I eat here for every lunch. Not only does it allow me to get out of the office for awhile, but I've been doing it for so long that I'm now treated like a regular. That means I get to exchange a lot of banter and visit with a variety of interesting people I've met here over the years. How many people do you know who can say they eat lunch regularly with a prostitute, a city councilman, the owner of a porno book-store, a lawyer, or an ex-con?

I never made it inside. Diane was sitting outside at one of the small tables on the sidewalk. I sat down opposite her. At least three guys inside pressed their faces to the glass and gave me a thumbs up sign. Diane and I had never been here to-gether before.

"I hope you're not mad," she said.

"About what?"

She swept her arm around. "Me being here. The way you've talked about this place, it almost sounds like family. I wasn't sure if you were ready to bring me home to meet mom."

I took her hand and helped her up. "Come on in and meet the family, dear. If you're good enough to sleep with, you're good enough to meet my kin."

She poked me in the ribs, so I entered the bar laughing. Someone yelled out, "He isn't going to need anything to drink for lunch!" The rest laughed.

I introduced her to everyone. The cook came out for a quick bow. The owner came downstairs from working on the books. The prostitute told Diane to look her up if she ever wanted to make some easy money.

I got a lot of ribbing from both the customers and the help, but eventually we were allowed to sit at a table next to the window and be left alone.

Diane's face glowed. "I love it. Would you mind if I ate lunch with you here once or twice a week?"

I squeezed her hand. "As often as you want." I didn't really mean that, of course. Like I needed Diane in my life, I needed these other people separate from her. A man has to have a social life, as limited as it might be.

She seemed to understand that. "No more than once or twice a week. The rest of the time I'll be having business lunches with people who can help my practice grow."

I tried not to look relieved. "Did you get lonely in that office all by yourself?"

"I was too busy to get lonely. I was on the phone all morning long. I've got three appointments lined up for this week already."

That was why she looked so excited. She had work. Those three appointments would get her maybe $120, enough to starve on in this town. "That's really great. In no time at all you will be so busy, I'll hardly see you."

She cringed. "All three are in the evening. In the beginning, most of my appointments will be at night. I'm afraid we won't always be seeing a lot of each other."

"You can come down and visit me during the day when work is slow."

That got a big smile from her. "I never thought of that."

It wasn't until we'd finished lunch that I told her about the e-mail message and my visit with Wilson. As usual, her training as a psychologist took over. After some thought, she said, "The lieutenant is probably right. The chances are pretty small that the message came from the shooter. I doubt he'll do anything that might expose him right now. In fact, I bet the shooting Saturday night gave him a good scare."

"And if you knew it was the shooter who sent the message, why do you think he'd do it?"

"That's easy. You've given him a scare."

"How could I scare him?"

"My guess would be that he has a lot of respect for computer technology, and he's afraid of your knowledge of it. If he doesn't leave any clues, cops can't catch him, but he might be afraid that somehow a computer could give him away."

That made perfect sense to me, and left me without an idea of what it meant. Other than the e-mail message, I hadn't come across anything to do with a computer that might link the two of us. Perhaps Diane and Wilson were both right. It was somebody else who wasn't happy with me.

"I don't feel any closer to solving this crime than I did in the beginning," I said.

Diane was thinking about something else. "You know," she said, "I've spent my life avoiding basketball players, and race car drivers, and bungi jumpers. I've always wanted someone safe. A regular guy with a good job who'd be there when I needed him. So what do I end up with? Some kind of crime fighter whose life has been threatened. I wonder what all that means?"

I was going to kid her about the observation until I realize she wasn't talking to me, but to herself. I paid for lunch and we walked back to the office building together.

SEVENTEEN

When I got into this business, I envisioned it as being white-collar all the way. I had no intention of sneaking around, breaking the law, or spying to get the information that people requested.

That certainly was a romantic notion, but not a very practical one. They call them secrets because people don't want you to know them. Those people might be relatives, neighbors, or—are you ready for this—government agencies there to serve your interests. Generally these folks only cough up information if you pay them enough or you find the right leverage.

I never was very good at strong-arm tactics, so I find being sneaky works best for me. That means I am not adverse to stretching the limits of the law a bit. I guess that makes me a radical. Heck, let's be honest. I'm a revolutionary radical. I don't mind breaking the law if it justifies the end.

I suppose that means I condone theft, breaking and entering, and general mayhem. Actually, I try to confine my misdeeds to electronic espionage. I don't mind breaking into computer systems to get the information I need, especially if that's the only way I know I'm going to get it. The law is a little vague on some of my activities because, let's face it, computer technology moves faster than government. Still, my attitude is pretty basic. If you don't want me in your computer records, do a better job keeping me out.

I'd prefer to do my work from the comfort and safety of my office, but sometimes I have to do what I'm doing tonight, which is sitting in an office with the blinds closed late at night, working only from a glow of a computer and my tiny flashlight.

No, this is not breaking and entering. Wade Stewart let me in. To arrange this, we played cute games. I entered the building dressed as a janitor. He sneaked back to the building wearing a rain coat with its collar turned up and a wide-brimmed hat with its brim turned down.

Who knows whether or not we needed to be this cautious? His blackmailer was getting really impatient. So much so that he'd wiped out another batch of files. I decided it was time to check out the computer itself, since Wade made all the changes I asked of him and still got hit.

I don't recommend taking apart a computer when the only illumination comes from a flashlight. When you drop things like screws, you tend to spend a lot of time on the floor crawling around looking for them.

I searched the insides of the computer from one end to the other to make sure nothing had been put inside that could trigger the virus. I even pulled the motherboard and replaced it with a new one to make sure that the ROM hadn't been touched.

Solving a computer problem is often a process of elimination. You have so many variables at work in the machine that you can't guess at the cause of something. Only by removing or replacing each element can you locate a problem. With the CD ROM installed the problem exists. With the CD ROM removed, the problem goes away. Bingo!

I'd played this game with Wade's system and found no Bingos! The virus wasn't in the machine. It had to be imported to do its job, and then disappear once it wiped out the files. That made my adversary one clever dude. Well, so was I.

I'd used the information from the backup tape Wade gave me to analyze the kinds of transactions that his company did by computer. They were pretty straight-forward. Folks wanted so many shirts, so many sweaters, and so many coats by such-and-such a date, to be paid in such-and-such a way. I wrote a program that would monitor each transaction, and, as long as it met the parameters set by it, would allow the data to be transferred. On the other hand, if the order had data in it that went outside the parameters, it would send out a message that said the transaction would have to be done by fax, by telephone, or by mail.

The next time the blackmailer tried to eliminate files by modem, he'd be in for a surprise. Just in case the blackmailer could break into the system, as some of us are apt to do, I buried this program so deep in hidden files that he'd have to spend hours on the computer to find it. Once he found that, he might possibly find the other little program I installed that recorded the times the computer was in use. If he tried to log-on after hours, I'd know about it. We'd just escalated the strategies of the game.

Wade and I got to go home before dawn. He'd covered himself by telling his secretary he had a golf game in the morning and not to expect him in until the afternoon, so he could sleep in. I wasn't so lucky: I'd found that most of Mark Whitlock's friends from law school and the majority of his family members, were on the east coast. I had some telephoning to do.

I was sitting at my desk making notes after finishing one

of my calls when Diane walked through on her way to her office. She paused long enough to put a cup of hot coffee on the desk for me and sniff my neck.

"Do I smell that bad?" I asked.

"No, but the other woman smells a lot like electrical stuff."

I laughed. I didn't tell Diane the details of what I was doing last night, only that I was doing some sensitive work for client who needed to be kept a secret, for now. I figured the less she knew about some of the work I did, the better. She wouldn't discuss her clients with me, nor would I expect her to. Although my privilege with my clients wasn't as protected as hers, I professionally thought I owed it to them to keep our work confidential. I'm not sure Diane agreed. She never said it, but I had noticed a twitch in her nose when I gave her vague answers about what I was doing.

"I haven't got a clue why a man would want two women, when one is more than he'll ever be able to handle."

She sat down on a bench and said, "I see you're working on a case involving child abuse."

I leaned back in my chair and sat quietly for a moment before lifting my eyes to hers. I saw what I was afraid I would see: I was about to face an inquisition from a pro-active counselor. "I'm not sure I can discuss this with you," I said.

Nice try, but she wasn't buying it. "If child abuse is an issue, it needs to be reported."

Legally, for her, there was some truth to that. I wasn't obligated the same way. "No charges were ever brought. Child abuse itself was never proven. So, why is it we're talking about this?"

"One," she said, "I'm a little disappointed you haven't said anything to me about this before now. You do know it's one of my areas of specialty and certainly one of my areas of concern. Two, we share a mutual client."

"Margorie Whitlock?"

"Margorie Whitlock."

"How is it you know her?"

"I met her at the club."

That made sense. Diane worked out several times a week at an athletic club near River Place. "And she happened to tell you about me."

"Like I said, she's a client. I can't exactly tell you what she's said. She does know about you, though, and she feels a little intimidated by you."

"I'm honored. I intimidate so few people."

"Don't be sarcastic. She's a very vulnerable woman right now, and she reads a threat into almost everything. You, apparently, have barely been cordial to her."

"We're not dating. I work for her. I'm not trying to build a friendship."

"She noticed."

"Without violating a trust, can you explain why she needs your services? She seemed to have it all pretty much together when I talked to her."

"Divorces are traumatic. You should know that. People don't get over them easily. Sometimes they need help."

"She's there to talk to you about divorce, but what you really want to talk about is child abuse."

She ignored any inferences I might have made. "What I want from you is Mark Whitlock's location when you find him, and I know you'll find him."

"Get the information from Mrs. Whitlock and make me feel better."

"She doesn't want me to know because she knows I'll report him to the authorities."

"She won't, but you will."

"Right."

"Maybe he's innocent."

She looked away and let out a long breath. I'd seen this Diane before. She was a volcano working overtime at not erupting. "Men are so predictable. They wink at prostitution. Affairs are worth high-fives in locker room. Sexual abuse of children has them looking the other way. Manhood is not a club for sexual predators."

I was tired and I wasn't in the mood for a feminist stereotype. "Diane, lighten up. I don't have the facts and I doubt if you do, either. If there is a crime to report, we'll deal with it when we know it's a crime. On the other hand, labeling all men as sexual perverts is not going to be good for business— your business, or the business of our relationship. I don't know Mark Whitlock from a shadow on a wall. I do know there is something I don't like about Margorie Whitlock. Like a good man in touch with his feminist side that I am, I'm going with my intuition until I'm proven wrong."

She tapped her foot and stared at me. Finally she said, "I hate it when you hide behind reason."

I shook my head. "I can't win, can I?"

"No."

"A woman thing. Right? You have to belong to the club."

"You got it."

"When this case is resolved and you've finished with your counseling of Mrs. Whitlock, we'll talk about it. For now let's see if we can avoid a conflict of interests. If we can't, then I'm going to have to drop Mrs. Whitlock as a client."

She stood up. "One of the things I like about you is that you can be so damned professional."

"Thank you," I said.

"It's also one of the things I don't like about you." She whirled around and left.

I mumbled at the door that closed behind her, "One of the things?"

Several hours later I was no closer to finding Mark Whitlock, no closer to identifying a blackmailer, and no closer to discovering the identity of a serial killer. I was disappointed, a little, beneath the glow of pleasure knowing that I wasn't just another computer geek but a guy who could make a difference.

EIGHTEEN

"This is stupid."

"It's got to be done, buddy. Blame Willie."

"Willie's an idiot."

"That's beside the point. He got his tag out so everyone can see it. If I don't do something about it, he's going to grab my title as Portland's best tagger."

"The title doesn't count for much if you're dead."

"Quit worrying. No one's been shot at for a week and a half. The guy's long gone."

The two of them stood at a base of a large billboard close to the freeway interchange that led either to downtown Portland or over the river to Washington. Two nights before, Willie had left his tag on the side of an overpass over a highway skirting Portland. He'd called Hal Arborstone shortly afterward to brag about the tag.

Hal had to concede that it was a masterstroke. Tagging an overpass that had traffic going under it constantly, even in middle of the night, was pretty daring. Doing it when the fear of the tagger killer was still at its peak was pure brilliance. The two boys had been competing with each other for years for the most number of tags left in the most daring of places. This last move put Willie up one. But not after tonight.

The billboard was on a spot that had one of the heaviest concentrations of traffic during the morning rush hours. Thousands of people would see his tag before veering left or right for west or east Portland. The only trick was doing it without getting caught. Even at three in the morning, cars were passing at regular intervals.

Hal had come prepared. To his friend, Steve, he said, "Give me the gun."

Steve rummaged in his backpack and then pulled out a pellet pistol. Four flood lights illuminated the billboard sign from overhead. With Steve as a lookout to signal when the road was clear of traffic, Hal sprang up and shot out each of the four lights.

"Is that going to be dark enough?" Steve asked, staring up at the shadowy billboard.

Hal looked across the road to the light that illuminated the freeway. He'd have liked to take that one out, too, but he didn't think the pellet gun had enough power to break through its lens. He'd have to risk it with it on. Besides, it gave him enough light to see what he was doing.

Welded on to one leg of the billboard was a metal ladder, making it easy for him to climb to the walkway below the advertisement for a locally brewed beer. The advertising featured a collection of gorgeous young people wearing the smallest of swimming suits at a beach scene which featured an ice-filled tub overflowing with bottles of the local beer. The young people looked delighted to be where they were.

Hal planned some modifications to the scene. Using his "Happy Rock" tag in creative ways, he planned to shape the letters into various pieces of anatomy. When he was done, none of the bathers would have suits. Instead they would have oversized genitalia shaped from the letters of his tag. He'd taken a picture of the billboard, and then he had spent a week making sketches and collecting paint to match colors.

He worked quickly but carefully, moving from one figure to the next. When he needed a new paint, Steve would throw a can up to him from the supply below. He finished just as a thin band of pale light appeared along the mountains to the east. He tossed the last can of paint down, hearing it thunk once as it hit, and then apparently bounce to thunk again.

"This is really great!" he said. "I'm dying to know how the news guys will cover *this,* because there's not a shot they can take of it they can show on television or put in the papers."

He climbed down the ladder to find backpacks and empty cans on the ground, but no Steve in sight. "The rat ran out on me," he said.

He gathered up all the cans and stuffed them into the packs. The last thing he wanted to do was leave something with his fingerprints on it. He'd been caught at this only once, but the cops had taken his prints as a precaution when they arrested him. Fortunately, he hadn't invented his new tag at that time, so they still didn't know who Happy Rock was.

They'd left the car several blocks away, on a road near the river. Hal figured Steve would be there.

He wasn't, though. He was a few feet away in the bushes where he had gone to urinate. He was still relieving himself when the bullet smashed his head and sent his body sprawling into a laurel, half on the ground and half suspended in air. He still held himself, urine dribbling out of his lifeless form.

Hal didn't see him. He'd moved back from the billboard as far as he dared without being obvious to the freeway traffic, so he could admire his work in the dim light. His appreciation was cut short when a slug smashed into the back of head and drove his body to the ground.

NINETEEN

I woke up with Diane curled in my arms, feeling very content with the world in general. So far, living together had been pure bliss. Buck was the only one not too happy about it. He'd been sent back to the far corner of the bed at night. He'd protested at first, sleeping outside at night, to show his displeasure. Until the next time it rained. Then he settled for the corner of the bed.

I stroked Diane's hair. She had a dozen clients now. That was far from being a successful practice, but after only two weeks, it was a remarkable number. She figured she would need at least 20 clients, half of them in for at least two hours a week, to make a go of it.

I wasn't sure what "a go of it" meant. Those 20 clients could bring in close to $60,000 a year. She would have office expenses, but no rent. That would leave her quite a bit of money left over. Did "a go of it" mean to have enough money to find a place of her own to live? I wished I knew the answer to that question, but I was afraid to ask.

We did manage to get out of bed. By Friday morning, I usually didn't have anything pressing to do, having worked my way through my jobs during the week. Diane still had most of her clients in the evenings, but now she had a couple that came in during the lunch hour twice a week, and one scheduled for ten on Saturday morning.

I wasn't excited about the Saturday morning clients, but she was right when she said that she would have to schedule Saturdays, especially if she was going to stick with theater. She'd have to make up for rehearsal nights and performances on Saturdays.

That made Friday mornings something special. We could stay in bed a little longer. We could make love and not worry about having the energy left to make it through the day. We could linger over breakfast and the newspaper.

I might have made it through the day without hearing about the shootings, but I turned on the local news on the radio while I dressed. I didn't have to hear many details before I was sure it was the same guy.

Earlier in the week I typed up all the information I'd given Wilson and sent it over in a "pretty" report to Curry. I still had time left on the contract with the police, but I'd already begun to feel that Curry and I should save the city money. Without some kind of clue, some kind of tip, or some kind of mistake, they weren't going to break this case. The Green River Killer had murdered more than forty times and then disappeared, uncaptured. This man had killed seven already and showed no signs of stopping.

Diane sat on the bed and listened to the radio report with me. When I turned off the radio, she asked, "What are you thinking?"

"I was thinking about the Green River Killer," I said. "He never got caught."

"Actually, he may have gotten caught for something else and is in jail. Or maybe one of his potential victims turned the tables and killed him and left his body in the woods to go undiscovered. Or maybe he died in a traffic accident."

"Or maybe he moved off some place else and has killed another forty people."

"The point is, if you don't want another mystery like the Green River one, solve this."

I looked at her and shrugged helplessly. "How?"

"You're Dataman. Figure it out." She bounced off the bed. "Got to go to work."

I leaned over the railing just as she was opening the apartment door and asked, "What will you do when you get those twenty clients?"

She looked back up at me, the blue eyes, the blonde hair, the clear complexion, the finely sculptured features ... I couldn't love her more than at this second, or at the one after it, or the thousands beyond. She smiled and her eyes took on a gleam. "I'll hire myself a secretary." And then she was out the door.

That was the answer I'd been afraid I wouldn't hear. It was a wonderful answer that inflated me with hope for the two of us. The joy carried into the next room. I sat down at my most powerful computer and said aloud, "Suppose the shooter is afraid of me and it's because of computers. What exactly do we have in here for him to fear?"

I went to the one place that might have the answer. I logged-on the Internet. There's not one thing the Internet can do that you can't do some other way: You can go to the porno bookstore and get the same X-rated pictures; you can pick up your phone and order airline tickets; you can go to the library and research material; but only on the Internet can you do it all from your keyboard without ever leaving your home and at a fraction of the cost it would take to do it any other way.

I can get current weather reports, stock market quotes, and movie reviews. I can play games. I can wander for hours and discover things I never imagined. I can "chat" about anything with someone sitting in a café in Germany with a computer also hooked up to the Internet. I can "chat." I can chat. I can chat?

Chat. An interesting word. One of the features of the Internet used by many are discussion groups. These groups cross the spectrum from high-brow to low-brow. If you have a hobby, you can hook into a group that shares your interests and chat with them. By chat, I mean typing conversations back and forth with each other. Dozens can participate and an unwritten protocol has been developed to control these discussions.

Doctors, lawyers, teachers, writers: all have discussion groups on the Net. I wondered if taggers, too, have a chat line?

It didn't take me long to find out—they did. Although taggers had to be somewhat cautious in a public forum like the Internet, that did not keep them from bragging about their exploits. Instead of using their names in the group, they use their tags. They also send samples of their work. That's how I saw the copy of the sketch that Hal Arborstone sent into his chat group, the one he'd sent in the day before he was murdered. It wouldn't have taken a rocket scientist to look at the sketch and know which billboard it was in Portland.

I'd never tried the computer chat lines before, and it showed. Each time I tried to wade in, I got rude messages back like SHUT UP, SHUT UP or GET OUT, GET OUT. Perseverance pays off, though. I finally got across the message that I was investigating the Portland tagger murders, and that two more had died last night, news my taggers in cyberspace didn't know. Of course they wanted the details. I gave the details in exchange for information I wanted.

That's how I found out about Happy Rock's sketch, which I downloaded and printed out, and about another Portland tagger, AC/BC, Brian Clark, the fifth boy to die. He, too, had bragged about his exploits before going out to do them.

Before I signed off with this group, I placed a note on their electronic bulletin board. It warned Portland taggers that the killer was on-line and monitoring their communications, if not participating in them as well. If they wanted to live, they needed to make sure they didn't tip their plans on the Internet.

I was positive now that the message in my e-mail was from the killer. I was sure this was part of what he didn't want me to find out, probably because the last thing he wanted was a warning like I had put on the bulletin board. Catching taggers in the act isn't easy. Just ask the police. It would be even harder for the killer, now.

Still, in the back of my mind I thought there had to be something else he didn't want me to know that I could find out through my computers. As much as I thought about it, though, I couldn't come up with a single idea. In a case like that, when I was stymied, I always switched directions and worked on something else. I liked to think my subconscious was working on the problem.

I did call Curry to let him know what I had discovered on the Internet. If he were a really clever fellow, he might try to trace the killer from the discussion group back to Portland. I would try, but it would take far more hours than I was being paid for, and I had other projects that needed to be done.

I also thought of trying to find out the names of people who had Internet access from Portland—for about a second. Too many variables. The killer could have direct access to the Internet, or he could have indirect access through a service provider such as CompuServe. Or he could be using the computer at work, or at school, or at the library, or at a café that served the Internet with coffee. Portland had three or four of those. Or he could be using someone else's computer. The possibilities were many and the chances of coming up with all the names impossible. It would have been nice, though, to see how many names showed up on the lists I had already made, cross-referenced with Internet access.

Curry was excited. My report hadn't impressed anyone, but this latest information would. He would investigate it as far as he could go. The Internet, though, he said, was a strange place, and no one was exactly sure how far his or her authority extended along it.

I suggested he try the FBI. The killer may have reached across state lines through the Internet to help him commit a crime. "I would think that would give the FBI some jurisdiction," I said.

"Wow," he said. "Wow. The thought is mind-boggling. We're in to whole new territory with this. I can't wait to throw these at our legal department and watch them have a cow. But first I'm going to call the Feds. I can see legal teams shoved into action all the way back to Arlington over this."

I said my goodbyes and thanked God those problems were his and not mine. I also decided that Diane and I wouldn't take any late-night trips for awhile, and I'd make sure the alarm system in the office was turned on every night, once we were in for good. If I had just thwarted the killer, I was pretty sure he wasn't going to be very happy with me. But, like most people who have lived a blessed life, I really didn't think he would come after me. Not Dataman.

TWENTY

I enjoy what I do—until it becomes work. I provide a complete written report for each of the jobs I do, whether or not I find the information requested. Even if I fail, I believe a report of my activities will keep the next guy from having to duplicate my work. The chase is fun. The aftermath is not. I've spent a good part of the day writing reports, including a new one for the police about what I found on the Internet. That's work.

Twice today I picked up the phone to call Margorie Whitlock to tell her I was off the case. Twice I put the phone down without completing the call. I used all sorts of arguments with myself to justify calling it quits, from conflict of interests because of my relationship with Diane, to too costly for me, considering I might spend dozens of hours trying to find her ex-husband with little chance of doing it.

Those would be lies, though, which explains why I didn't make the calls. The truth is I don't like Margorie Whitlock, and I don't trust her. I started to distrust her when I discovered she hadn't told me about the charges of sex abuse. That distrust was confirmed when I found out how she had met Diane. Margorie had gone up to her in the gym to introduce herself after she'd become my client.

Portland's not that big a place, and it's possible for a

client of mine to run into the woman I see, but it'sn't so likely she'd turn to Diane for counseling, considering how little time Diane has been in the business, and how little advertising she's been able to do. I was convinced that Margorie had sought her out. But why?

I decided that I might have a better chance to find Mark Whitlock if I knew more about Margorie Whitlock. I spent more of my day in research, only I didn't think Margorie was going to pay me for it.

Computers are a bit like Chinese puzzle boxes. If you have to sit and stare at one from across the room, the chance are excellent that you won't find out what's inside. But, if you can get your hands on it, you have a chance of getting the box open. Getting your hands on a computer can be done several ways. I'd already gotten a good look at Wade Stewart's computer by seeing his backup tape. I got even more intimate with it when I pried off the lid and poked around inside. I got a deeper look into it when I sat at its keyboard and examined its files.

A good hacker doesn't even need to see a computer to get into it. A modem will do the trick. But even good hackers can't get into most secure systems no matter how good he or she is. That trick is left to a few very elite people. Someone who, say, started his career in the Silicon Valley designing advanced computers systems, someone who acted as a consultant for new operating systems, and someone who critiqued the designs of the latest chips. That trick is for someone who really knows how a computer works, which means someone who knows all the methods that can be created to keep people from getting inside it.

I moved to the Silicon Valley to Hewlett Packard. I'm still called occasionally by both companies I worked for to get my thoughts about new designs. They send me schematics and I get to write more reports. I charge both companies a hundred dollars an hour for my services. I smile every time I make out a bill. It's through these two contacts more than anything that has kept me current on how to break into computers.

By day's end I'd discovered quite a bit of information about Margorie Whitlock, most of it confusing. I was suppose to find her ex-husband because she desperately needed his support payments. Considering that she drives a Mercedes, that her daughter goes to a private school, that she just recently paid for her condo in cash, and that she has investments, savings and checking accounts worth three million dollars without one single debt against her, I was having trouble understanding why she needed her husband's money.

Anger and a desire for revenge have a place in a messy divorce. She certainly was in a position to vent anger and get revenge when she held her husband hostage by the threat of charging him with child abuse. He seemed to have squirmed off the hook she'd set, so I might understand why she wanted him found—she wasn't done playing the line and reeling him to the boat. Only, she didn't seem angry to me. She seemed nervous. Her husband had thrown the hook. Did she think she was trying to land a great white and now it was lurking just below the surface, always a threat to strike back?

I didn't know, but, of course, I'm the guy who'll play with a Chinese puzzle box until I can get it open, and I'll probe a computer until I can find my way into its internal works. A guy like that won't throw back a case just because he doesn't like or trust a client. Not when he's become curious.

Besides, I had a copy of Tamera Whitlock's file right out of her psychologist's computer. Folks who deal with such sensitive material really ought to do more to protect it. I blush at my audacity, but I know one thing for sure: I'll do a better job of protecting Tamera's confidentiality than her psychologist, a Ms. Denise Britt. She's up next for a background check.

I had just started to shut down the computers when the phone rang. I picked it up on the third ring. I immediately lost a little hearing to the booming voice of a very irate Wade Stewart. "The son of a bitch did it again! He wiped out more files on the computer and gave me until tomorrow to pay up or he'll destroy the rest. Listen, Walkinshaw, you promised me you'd done something about this. What kind of a quack are you?"

I kept the phone a foot away from my ear until I could only hear heavy breathing. I said, "Wade, you won't have to pay a penny." I gave him some very precise instructions to gather some information for me and to drop it off on his way home.

After I had hung up, I leaned back in my chair feeling exhausted. Sometimes you work like hell to get into that Chinese puzzle box because you're sure that the spot of microfilm is located inside. You're so busy trying to get inside you fail to notice the dot on the "i" in the word "price" on the tag has fallen off and floated away. You guessed it—the microfilm. I had come pretty damned close to blowing this one because I hadn't thought about the dot on the "i."

TWENTY-ONE

After my busy day, I was having one of those evenings of great reflection. I was leaning back on the sectional with my feet on the coffee table. I had the lights low and James Taylor singing sweetly in the background. I had a good cup of coffee cradled in my lap.

I needed the time to relax. The information that Wade Stewart had dropped off was on my desk. I was already afraid of what I'd find. Wade wouldn't like it; neither would I. If I was right, a lot of people would be hurt.

I felt differently about the Whitlock case. I had a sneaky feeling about it, one I hoped wasn't going to be true. If it was, then my idiotic blind faith in the notion that man was predominately good would take another hit.

I was looking forward to Diane coming down from work. I needed her tonight. I could not believe how much more content I was now that she lived with me. She added some unidentifiable element to my life that hadn't been there before. Now, when I walked into the apartment it was with the anticipation of seeing her, instead of quiet and solitude. For the most part, I worked alone all day long; I really didn't need to go home to solitude. But tonight, she'd picked up another client at the last minute and Sunday night was the only time they could meet.

I leaned forward to put my cup on the coffee table. I felt it before I heard any noise. It was like a big hand had taken a vicious swipe at my head, only it had missed, just barely, and my hair had flown from the breeze it caused. Instinctively I kept rolling forward until I fell off the sofa onto the floor.

I'm not sure I could describe the sound. First was a *twink*, followed by a louder *thunk*. I raised my head over the sofa to look. Where my head had been only moments before was a hole in the window that looked like it had been make by a fist punched through the glass. I followed an invisible line to the office wall. The plaster was caved in at about the same height. The hole looked like it had been made by a bowling ball.

I knew it wasn't a bowling ball. A high-powered rifle had fired a homemade slug with a X'd-over hollow point. If I hadn't leaned forward at the instant I had, I'd have been another victim of the shooter.

The lighting in the apartment was dim. The gauze curtains made it difficult to see inside. The darkness would have made it impossible. Even his night scope wouldn't have done the trick. He had to have an infrared scope. That was the only way he could have picked me out in here.

Lights out, lights on. It didn't make any difference. His scope would pick up my body heat. I could set the place on fire to confuse him, but the problem with that was I'd probably burn myself to a crisp.

For the moment I was stuck.

I could tell by the way the two holes lined up that he was on the top floor of a two-story parking garage kitty-corner from my apartment. The garage was kept very dark at night. It was used for night-time parking when there was a major production at the Performing Arts Center or Civic Auditorium, but for the most part it was locked up and kept dark in the evenings. During the day it was filled with cars of the people who worked in the area.

That meant the shooter wouldn't be in too big a hurry to leave, unless he heard sirens. He didn't have to worry about anyone else in the garage stumbling across him.

And he didn't have to worry about police sirens. At the moment I couldn't get to the phone. I was safe where I was, but there weren't too many other places I would be safe. He was at the same height as my apartment. He could see any movement through the scope. I guessed he'd try to move a little higher, maybe by standing on the wall around the top of the lot. If he did, he'd have a shot at me if I tried to crawl to the kitchen or to the door.

I did not feel fear. Not yet. I knew, though, I had tickled the dragon's tail and now I faced the hot breath. He must have logged-on and read the bulletin board. Maybe he spent last night cruising for some taggers and didn't find any. Maybe he had a whole day to get really pissed off about it. Maybe he'd decided I was getting too close. I hoped I'd be around to find out.

I glanced at my watch. *That's* when I felt fear—Diane was due back any minute. I couldn't stay curled up here and wait. As soon as she walked through the apartment door, he'd have a clear shot at her.

I rolled on my back and scooted under the coffee table. I started to slide out the other side in hopes of getting to the door when there was another *twink*, followed by a series of *thunks*. The top of the coffee table was made from a thin, polished granite slab set on an iron frame. The bullet had ricocheted off the top, shrapneling around the room after impact.

That gave me an idea: I pushed up on the frame of the table

with all my strength; I was just able to lift it. Lifting with my heals dug in, I was able to drag the table forward and over the top of me. If I could do it ten times, I'd make it to the door.

He fired three more shots before I got the table near the door. I stayed on my back under the table, trying to figure out how I could reach up and open the door without being shot. He would have a clear shot at me for a brief moment.

I stopped worrying about it when I heard Doris' voice announcing that I had e-mail. Diane had entered the office and turned on the lights. I shot out from under the table, grabbed the door knob, ripped open the door and flung myself through the opening, yelling the whole time for Diane to get down.

For a brief second she must have thought I was insane. But only for a brief second. Another *thunk* sent the door slamming shut.

I was on the floor, under a computer table. "Grab the phone and get behind the desk!" I shouted. "I'm being shot at!"

Thank God she was an actress used to taking direction. She grabbed the phone and dropped without a second thought.

I was pretty sure we were both safe where we were. From where he was, he could see only the front part of the office. The corner of the building across the street would block his view of some of it, as would the wall between the office and the apartment.

I could hear Diane call the police. She sounded very calm as she explained the situation and gave directions. As soon as she hung up, the one computer monitor on in the room exploded.

"Oh, Tom," Diane cried out, "He's shot Doris!"

I started to laugh, and then she started to laugh, too. We were both still laughing when we heard the first sirens. I was sure, as police cars began to pull up, that the shooter was gone. I crawled out from under the desk and picked up a small fire extinguisher, which I kept on each of the computer tables. I stepped over and made sure the monitor wouldn't set the office on fire. In an instant the fire extinguisher was gone and I stared down at blood on the back of my left hand. I didn't understand.

"Drop!" Diane screamed.

I might have made a good actor. I dropped on cue. Another computer monitor exploded.

Neither one of us moved again until the cops started shouting at us through the office door. Diane crawled over and unlocked it to let them in. They came in like a combat team, with guns drawn, each backing up the other as they slipped into the room. They simply motioned us to stay where we were and continued to work their way through the office and into my apartment. A few minutes later one of them came out of the apartment and said it was okay to get up.

I was glad to get up. My hand hurt. But when I stood, I almost went over again—my knees were weak. I don't know if it was from loss of blood or fear, but my body was starting to shut down. Diane was quickly at my side and helped me to sit down in the recliner.

The back of my left hand and two spots higher up on my arm were ripped open. The shooter had tried until the last possible second to get me. The one shot that did connect had ricocheted off a window frame, deflecting it enough so that most of it hit the fire extinguisher, the rest hitting my arm. If it hadn't been for the window frame, I would have taken the shot chest high.

Paramedics arrived shortly after the police. They determined that the tears to my body looked worse than they were, and I wasn't in any immediate danger. I would have to stop by the hospital later for stitches, but for now I could stay and talk to the police.

We had a lot of police. Wilson and Curry showed up at the same time. Diane tried to make coffee for them all at first, but then she ran out of cups, followed by coffee.

Wilson took one look at all the activity in my office and said, "Let's talk in the hall."

"I have an office upstairs," Diane offered. To me she said, "And more coffee."

Her office was a treat. It was tastefully decorated. The furniture was expensive. She added each day nice touches like freshly cut flowers and candy made daily in a store down the block. Diane and I sat down together on the sofa. Curry and Wilson sat down in armchairs at opposite ends of the office from each other.

Curry had a look of pure ecstasy on his face. "This is great," he said.

Wilson glared at him, and then looked at me and asked, "Great?" I shrugged. I didn't know what he was talking about.

"Great," Curry repeated. "Your trip on the Internet seems to have gotten instant results."

"My trip on the Internet damned near got me killed."

This time Wilson glared at me. "What trip?"

"I'm feeling a little weak," I said. "Curry, you explain." Actually, the threat behind Wilson's glare made me feel weak.

Curry explained about what I had found on the Internet. Then he told us he'd logged-on, too, and, after making contact with several people in the discussion group, was sure the shooter had used them to pick out targets in Portland. Several people remembered one person on-line who called himself Chemical Waste, who was particularly interested in where everyone was from.

"I'm sure," Curry said, "that this confirms that the shooter used the Internet."

"More than anything," Wilson said, "it confirms that Walkinshaw here has pissed him off. A man who stands his ground and keeps firing even when police cars are pulling up sounds plenty mad to me."

"I don't see why somebody didn't catch him," Diane said.

"If you'd told us on the phone that someone was shooting at you from the parking garage," Wilson said, "we might've caught him. You gave the address and said someone was shooting at you. Forgive the officers if they thought the shots were coming from inside the building instead of outside."

In Diane's defense, I said, "But the shooter wouldn't have known what she called in. He didn't know the cops wouldn't come right to the parking garage. Did he want me that dead to put himself at risk?"

Diane immediately got up to get a note pad and pencil. I'd started her wheels turning. "While I'm up, does anyone want coffee?" We all did.

Curry said, "I think it's because you made him mad."

"Or he's stupid," Wilson said.

"Or he doesn't care if he gets killed," Diane added.

"She's a psychologist," I said.

"Another worthless profession," Wilson said.

"So, I won't use you for a reference," Diane said to him. "Believe it or not, this adds a lot to what you know about the man. I think we can emphasize man here, and not boy. He's simply too knowledgeable and skilled to be some kid or some gang member. He can manipulate others on the Internet. He can make his own bullets. He's got some kind of a silencer on the rifle, probably homemade, and Tom is sure he was using an infrared scope this time, instead of a night scope. A night scope wouldn't have allowed the shooter to see through the curtains; only an infrared one would.

"Also, he doesn't scare easily. He's still willing to shoot at his target with cops swarming around. Usually, people who don't scare easily, don't have a whole lot of respect for life, theirs or others."

"Fascinating," Wilson said with undisguised sarcasm. "I'll be sure to read it when it comes out in paperback."

"I'm interested," Curry said.

Encouraged, Diane continued. "I doubt that he's getting much satisfaction from these killings. He might get a short rush, but I suspect that even now he knows it isn't going to make him feel better for long. He may have thought the killings were the answer to his problems in the beginning—he doesn't anymore. That's why he doesn't care if he gets killed or not."

"That should make our job easier," Wilson said. "Maybe he'll even paint a target on his chest."

"No targets," she said. "But up until now, he's been pretty careful and pretty secretive. Expect him in the future to be more confrontational. Next time he might hang around long enough to get in a shoot-out with the cops. He might try anything to capture the initial rush he felt when he killed the first tagger."

"What makes you so sure you're right?" Wilson asked. "What makes you so sure he got such a rush the first time?"

"Because he killed a second and a third and a fourth and a fifth and a sixth and a seventh victim. Because he's tried to get a couple of more and missed. He wouldn't keep doing it if he didn't think it was going to make him feel good."

"How about the guy is crazy? That's all. He's crazy. You can't explain why a crazy person does what he does."

"Mr. Wilson," Diane said, "the only difference between you and a crazy person is you don't think the same way; therefore, you don't behave the same way. Go back to the police station and look at your mug books. Most of the people in them don't look like criminals. The shooter isn't going to look like a killer. He's going to look a lot like you, only he doesn't think the same way."

"And why doesn't he think the same way?" Curry asked.

"Genetics, brain damage, or severe trauma. Those are the things that usually alter normal behavior."

"So which of the three has done this guy in?" Wilson asked.

"My guess would be severe trauma," Diane said. "Otherwise you'd've heard from him long before this. I'd look for someone who's already wound tight who had something, or maybe a series of somethings, hit him all at once and push him over the edge."

"What kind of somethings?" Curry asked.

"If he's wound tight, the incidents might seem fairly harmless to us. Maybe someone sprayed his new car; maybe someone threw a rock through his picture window. He might be targeting taggers, but he may have a grudge against teen vandals in general. When he shot at Tom, we knew he wasn't going to stay exclusive when it came to targets."

Not much else was said after Diane served the coffee. The two took notes about what happened in the apartment and office. When Wilson was done, he got up to leave. He paused long enough to stick a finger in my face. "Butt out," he said. "This no longer concerns you. I'll see to it you get the message in writing from the department. If you continue, I'll see that you get arrested for interfering with a police investigation." He slammed the door behind him for emphasis.

Curry insisted on driving us the hospital to have my wounds stitched. He waited the two hours it took and drove us back to the office. He even insisted on walking us all the way back to the apartment to make sure we didn't run into any surprises along the way.

At the door, Curry said, "Forgive Wilson if he seems to be upset about all this. He believes civilians who get in the way of police work deserve whatever happens to them. I'm not of the same school. Your building will be under police surveillance twenty-four hours a day. You're not to travel anywhere without letting us know in advance. Your car will be followed by a squad car. I'm also going to arrange for an emergency line directly to the station so you won't have to do any more than pick up your phone and hit the pound sign to get immediate response."

"Do you think all that's necessary?" Diane asked.

"I do now," he said, shutting the door behind him.

Diane and I stood in the open doorway of the apartment and surveyed the damage in both rooms. "I'll get some people in tomorrow to fix the windows and walls," I said.

"What about Doris?"

I looked at the shattered monitor. "I don't want you to ever bad mouth Doris again—she saved your life."

"If you can save her, I promise I won't."

"I'll have to check out the system in the morning, but I think most of the damage was done to the monitors. Regardless, I can replace whatever was damaged with extras I have here. We'll be back to normal by noon."

She looked at my arm. "Can it ever be back to normal?"

I let out a breath I think I had been holding for most of the evening. "I suppose you want to go someplace else."

"Where are you going to be?"

"I'm staying right here," I said. "The asshole is going to have to kill me to keep me from doing anything different."

"If this is where you're going to be, then this is where I'm going to be."

I shook my head and felt a flush I thought would turn to tears. "I appreciate that," I said, my husky voice giving away my emotions.

She took my good hand. "Do we get a gun?"

"I don't like them," I said.

"I don't like them, either."

"What do you think the chances are he'll come back?"

"For now, I don't think you'll have to worry; you were never one of his primary targets. You just got in his way. When he reads in the paper that you got shot, that should satisfy his need for revenge, or, more likely, punishment. As long as you stay out of his way ..." She looked at me, the question in her eyes. Was I going to stay out of his way?

"For now we put the place back in order and let the police do their jobs. Then we'll see. The first thing I'm going to do is replace those curtains with blinds, ones that can be closed up so tight at night that neither infrared or night scopes will make a difference."

Just then Buck popped through a hole in the glass and landed on the back of the sofa. He surveyed the mess and then looked at us like we had a lot of explaining to do.

"Where was he when we needed him?" I asked.

"I don't know, but do you think we could teach him karate?"

"We need to do something. He's a lousy watch cat."

TWENTY-TWO

For two weeks now, no one has died, at least at the hand of the man who hates taggers. The police report that tagger-graffiti has almost disappeared. They say the few paintings reported have taken place during the daylight hours and most of those taggers have been identified and caught.

I've received two e-mail messages from the killer. The first one said: Sorry I missed. The second read: Don't give me reason again to kill you. Jokingly, I asked Curry if he thought that was a threat. He said, no, he was pretty sure it was more like a promise.

I wrote up my final report and submitted it to the police to earn the last of my fee. Curry said they were pretty happy with what they got, even if they hadn't caught the killer yet. He was still working the Internet, where he felt he'd ultimately track down the killer.

The Net is a big place. I was sure it'd take some wizardry I didn't know to trace the killer on it. I still felt something to do with computers was the key to the case, but I didn't know what it was, but it didn't have to do with the Internet. Knowing about the Net only made it harder for the killer to find victims; it didn't lead us back to him.

One day we had police protection, and then we didn't. I'd

gotten used to them being around, so I noticed immediately when they weren't. I called Curry about it. The only thing he could tell me was that the stopping of the patrols had been Wilson's call. Apparently he no longer thought my life was threatened. I wished I felt that way, too.

Diane and I were moving into June with things looking bright for both of us. Diane sold the condo and paid off the office, even having some money left over. She has been talking about the two of us getting a bigger place someday. She even suggested that if we had enough room, my children might not mind staying with us in the summer.

She says a lot of things like that, mostly I think to reassure me that we are doing OK. together. Unfortunately, she's never met my children. They haven't yet had to deal with another woman. Their mother, bless her confused heart, once divorced from me, has only dated occasionally and hasn't had a serious relationship. Apparently, affairs are only fun if you're married. At any rate, the fact that the two of us seem unattached, the children harbor hope that we'll get back together again. They'll discover the truth when they meet Diane.

I took Diane's suggestion and called around to the computer related companies in the Portland/Beaverton area and told them I planned on taking short trips to California on a regular basis, and I was interested in doing some consulting, seeing if there were some services that the Silicon Valley and the Electronic Forest could share with each other. I was surprised by the response. It was universally positive. When I made contacts with companies in California I got the same response. The companies like the idea of an independent trying to bridge the gap between them—they don't trust each other enough to try it themselves.

I set up several appointments at companies in Oregon for the month of June. I made more appointments over a two-week period in July, in California, when I'd be down to see my kids. Risking two weeks away from work was a gamble, but if these contacts paid off, the financial reward would far outweigh the time away from work.

I was also worried about being away from Diane for two weeks. She told me she had no intention of not seeing me for two weeks; she'd take a long weekend in the middle of my trip and fly down to see me. She thought I should let the kids know about her before she came down, and then the four of us should spend some time together. She also said she didn't expect a warm reception from them, and I should not, either.

Considering that only two weeks earlier I was inches from being dead, bleeding from wounds, and knowing what it was like to be a fox in a hound hunt, a lot had changed for me in that time. Except one thing. I still wanted to find the killer.

I was sitting at one of my computer stations, switching from one view to another on the monitor, when Diane walked in. "Want to go to lunch?" she asked.

I glanced at my watch. I'd been so wrapped up in my own thoughts, I'd forgotten about lunch. "Sure, but let me show you this first." I switched back to the first screen.

She looked at it for a second, and then said, "That's the front entrance to the building."

I switched the screen two more times. "This second one is the side entrance, and the third is the service entrance. This cost me a few bucks out of my pocket, but I had cameras installed and a wireless relay to send the signals up here to this computer. I have an electronic sensor on each of the doors. Any time one opens, or even if enough pressure is put on one of the locked doors, the computer will beep and automatically switch to the camera on that door."

"Wow. You did that yourself?"

"All by myself."

"What have the other owners said?"

I laughed. "They'll be getting a note from me that says I've installed, at my own cost, a camera security system in the building, and I'll be glad to hear from them if they have any concerns."

"Let me see, you've done something to make the building more secure and it hasn't cost me a penny. I'm going to complain, right?"

"I'm counting on no one complaining."

"People can be strange creatures. You might have someone in the building who'll see it as an invasion of privacy."

"If they're coming back late at night to have an affair, I could understand that. But after the shooting here, I think most of the other owners won't question the addition of security cameras."

"We should get together for a meeting sometime and get to know each other and see what kinds of concerns the other owners have."

"Sure," I said. "We'll have a block party."

We each paid a certain amount of money every month into a maintenance fund for the building itself, and we each contracted for our own cleaning services. At the end of the year, the owners were notified of his or her share of the property tax assessment on the building. In some ways, owning our own offices wasn't much different than renting them. As a result, we saw little need to meet with each other, except to nod and to smile as we passed in the hallways.

She sat down in the recliner. Within seconds Buck appeared on the window sill, squeezed under the open window, and climbed into her lap. "How's work going?"

This may have seemed like a casual question, but she had an agenda buried beneath it. She really wanted me to drop the investigation of the tagger killings. She didn't say it out loud, but the shooting incident had shaken her more than me. She didn't want it to happen again.

Neither did I. On the other hand, I was a man who loved to solve problems, and this was a big problem. "I'm caught up for the week." This was one of the good weeks. I've billed for 44 hours of work, but I've put in about 36 hours of actual time. Even if a job takes less than an hour of my time, I still bill for the full hour. My contract makes that clear. This week I had quite a few jobs that took less than an hour. My reward was an afternoon free.

"I wish I could say I was," she said. "I've got clients from one to seven this afternoon, nonstop."

"I'll make a dinner reservation for us for eight, and then we can catch a late movie at the KOIN Center."

"How about Greek?"

"There's that place on, what, Fifth?"

"I think it's Fifth. We can walk to the KOIN building from there."

"Do you still want to go to lunch?"

"I was thinking," she said. "We could go get hamburgers."

We settled for hamburgers down the block and came back just in time for Diane's next appointment. I kissed her goodbye and gave her enough time to disappear upstairs before I locked my office door and slipped out of the building. I didn't want her to know I was going back to Fremont High School.

The decision had not come easily, but I didn't like getting shot—it played too roughly with my illusion of immortality. On the other hand, I don't like defeat. Not at my game in my arena. The shooter had come here to stop me. I resented that. And, finally, I still couldn't answer the question of why the shootings started at Fremont. There had to be some kind of a connection. A man doesn't just decide to kill taggers one day, and then go out that night and, surprise, surprise, find two of them at work right where he happens to be. The killer, some-how, knew the taggers would be there. And, for some reason, the fact that they were tagging the school was the last straw for him. He flipped out and killed.

But it wasn't as easy as that. He had a weapon that showed preparation. Homemade bullets. Homemade silencer. Night scope. The idea of killing someone, maybe not even taggers, had come to him well before the night he first killed. When the opportunity arrived, he was ready for it. But how did he know about the opportunity? If I could answer that, I could nail him.

I drove to Fremont in the Healey with the top down. Oregonians are a strange lot. They complain a lot about the rain, but they only get about a third of what folks in Florida get. Snow turns streets into a destruction derby, but they long to see it fall at least once each year. And, when the sun comes out as it had today, they worship it more than the Arizonians, or the Californians, or the Floridians. They worship it as a precious commodity only guaranteed during the summer months and a bonus any other time. The sun was out and my top was down. I was one of those worshippers.

The parking lot in front of the school was filled. I had to squeeze into space meant for motorbikes. I climbed out of my car and stood for a long time simply staring at the building. I was trying very hard to see something I hadn't seen before.

I hadn't taken more that twenty steps toward the building when the front door opened and Ms. Cray came marching out. She greeted me in the parking lot with, "That parking space is reserved for motorcycles only."

"It's good to see you again, Principal Cray. I'm sorry if I parked in the wrong spot, but it's the only one I could find."

"We have visitor parking on the other side of the building."

"Do you want me to move my car?"

"I want to know why you're here. I wasn't notified by the police you'd be coming."

"I've spent a lot of hours investigating the shootings. I still haven't been able to figure out why they started here. I thought I'd come back to see what I missed."

"This is a very busy time for us," she said. "The seniors have their last day tomorrow, graduation is next week, and then the others will be out at the end of following week. We don't have time for you. I hope you can understand that."

"I hadn't intended to come in the building," I said. "I just wanted to see if there was something I missed."

"All of this has been thoroughly investigated."

I pointed to the roof. "Are those security cameras?"

She didn't even look in the direction I was pointing. She said, "Yes. We have a half a dozen of them on the roof. They're sensitive to movement. If something moves, they start recording. We use them at night, or we switch them on during the day when we see something suspicious outside, like you, Mr. Walkinshaw."

I smiled and waved at the camera. "Are they new?"

"No. We've had them for several years."

"Then they must have recorded the shooting."

"Mr. Walkinshaw, you're far behind the police investigation. That was one of the first things they asked about."

"And?"

"I really should refer you to the police on this."

"You'll get rid of me faster if you tell me yourself."

She needed little convincing beyond that. "They went on the blink that night. They weren't recording during the time of the shooting."

Behind her, behind the closed doors of the school, I could see someone watching us. I thought it might be the security guard. "Do they go on the blink often?"

"Only rarely. The police think the fog might have somehow shorted them out."

"That makes sense," I said. "By the way, who's that in the doorway?"

She glanced back. When she turned her head, the figured turned away and left. "I can't tell," she said.

"I suppose it was a security guard or a student."

"Neither," she said. "We don't let students out of the classroom except during passing time during the last days. It cuts down on the number of problems we might have. One security guard called in sick today, and I have the other out in the back parking lot. We had some car break-ins there yesterday afternoon. That's why I spotted you: I was keeping an eye on the front parking lot."

"Thanks," I said. "It's a shame about the cameras. If they'd worked, several teens might still be alive."

"If those teens had not decided to break the law, they would still be alive, as well."

I waved and left. I didn't want to get into an argument with her about whether or not taggers deserved the death penalty.

I took the long way back. I drove down 99 through Oregon City, enjoying the winding road along the river. I cut across to the freeway from Canby, and then I drove back into Portland. By the time I put it away, the car had gotten a good run.

Back in my office I began a task I wanted to avoid. It was not only time-consuming for me, it also tied up several of the computers. I loaded in the names of the faculty members, and then I wrote a program to run those names through whatever police records or other files that involved legal action I could access. I didn't expect to get much: In Oregon, when teachers applied for, or renewed, a teaching certificate, their finger-prints were run to check for criminal records.

I had a bigger problem when I loaded in the student names. Records were sealed for juveniles. That didn't mean I wouldn't find something. Newspapers were free to run names of juvenile offenders if they could get them and if they chose to do so. Most papers ran the names of teens charged with major crimes. About the only thing I could do here was to write a program to cross-reference any news articles in the last few years of the *Oregonian*. The *Oregonian* had been on-line with back issues since then. Both programs instructed the computer to print out what-ever they found, so two computers and printers would be tied up for most of the weekend for these tasks.

Diane and I had a great evening together. The Greek din-ner was spicier than I liked it, but the food was different from my normal fare and challenged my taste buds. We saw a new movie that had received great reviews that neither of us liked, which made it perfect for us. We had a lively discussion about its flaws afterward at the Metro over decaffeinated coffee and gooey pastry.

Back in the office, I checked the two computers to see

how they were doing. One was huffing and puffing, leaving a large stack of printouts behind. I looked through a few and discovered they were positive stories about student accomplishments. I hadn't thought about that, and there was no way for me to get the program to just print out bad things about teens. I put more paper in the laser printer for that computer. The other computer had fewer sheets.

I wasn't interested in going through these things now. Diane had gone into the apartment, telling me she was going to take a shower.

I moved to the computer with the camera system on it. A little box was flashing green in the upper left-hand corner of the blank screen. This system, too, had a sleep mode, and only came to life when it was given a task, like the doors opening downstairs. I had programmed it so that any doors opening, or any attempt to open the doors after closing time, which was at eleven at night during the week and six at night on the weekends, would cause the cameras to come on and record what they saw, digitizing the images and storing them on this computer. If everything worked, the flashing green light meant that the computer had recorded Diane and me returning from the movie.

I went to the file with the stored recording and hit PLAY. I was expecting to see the two of us, but what I saw startled me. A man in an overcoat and a hat pulled low over his eyes approached the side door of the building. He gave the doors a shove. When the doors didn't open, he gave them even a harder shove. The camera picked up their rattling sound. He glanced up, caught sight of the camera inside the building, ducked his head and hurried away. The camera view switched to the front of the building. It showed Diane and me returning. Those were the only two clips.

I replayed the first clip. Two things bothered me about it. When the man glanced at the camera I couldn't see much of his face, but it reminded me of the man standing in the doorway at Fremont High. The second thing that bothered me was the time: The man had been here only a few minutes before we returned.

I made sure all the security systems were in place, and I went around to close all the blinds tightly. The last thing I did was shut Buck's window. I hoped he was inside already or he'd have to spend the night on the roof.

When we crawled in bed, I made sure the phone was on the bed stand. Diane didn't notice; since the shooting, the phone had gone to bed with us every night.

By the way, Buck crawled on the bed just as we were settling down. I was glad I hadn't locked him out. I had this fear the shooter would go after anything to hurt me, like Buck—or Diane.

TWENTY-THREE

While Diane met with her Saturday morning clients, I began going through the printouts from the computers. The staff search was done. The student search was still running.

As I expected, I didn't find any significant crimes attached to any of the staff members. I did find an interesting tidbit or two: The art teacher had applied for a marriage license; an English teacher had been arrested for drunken driving a second time; the science teacher's wife had filed for a divorce; the Ag. teacher and his wife, who was the librarian, had filed for adoption of a newborn; a social studies teacher was buying a new house; and one of the counselors had a restraining order out against a former boyfriend. For the most part, the kinds of legal dealings these folks had pretty much matched the legal dealings of most folks.

Ms. Cray did not show up on any of the paperwork. I wasn't surprised. I imagined that administrators went through an even tighter screening than staff members.

I'd hoped to spot something that would set off alarm bells. I didn't, so I went to the next step. I used the yearbook to examine staff photos. I went through the mug shots, and then I went through candids of the staff in the book. I didn't see one who looked like the man on the tape, but that didn't mean much—I hadn't seen his face.

I thought we might stay in tonight so I could watch the monitor to see if the guy came back again. If he did, that would certainly tell me something.

I also tried to be objective and pragmatic. The guy in the doorway at school and the guy on the video could have been two different people. The guy at school could have either been a student or a staff member curious as to why the principal was out in the parking lot talking to some man. The guy in the video might not have been looking up at the camera at all, since a clock was mounted close to it. Instead of quickly fleeing the camera, he might have noted the time on the clock and realized the building was closed for the night. I reminded myself that people who got shot probably became paranoid.

A first look at the stack of papers on the students showed me what I was afraid it would: Other than a few students getting shot or hurt in auto accidents, little of the information was negative. In fact, Fremont High was filled with some remarkable students who excelled in academics, sports, and good deeds.

That brought me back to zero. At least on paper. My gut still told me that the clue was at Fremont High. Logic told me we were dealing with an adult, not a student. Instinct said that that adult was somehow connected to the high school.

But how? Who wouldn't show up in the annual who might be standing in the doorway of the school? A teacher new this year. A volunteer. A parent stopping by the office. I'd have to find out, which meant another visit to the school. This time I'd try to get Curry to call ahead for me and clear the way.

I looked at the staff pictures again. I reminded myself that Ted Bundy looked liked the clean-cut kid next door. He was a law student; a volunteer in the election campaign for governor; well-liked and respected by those who knew him. And he murdered more than thirty women.

One of the nice-looking people on the staff may have already killed seven people and was just getting started.

Stymied for the time being, I returned to the two other cases that had me perplexed. I called Wade Stewart and told him that in a few days I'd want to meet with him in the office. I also wanted to meet with the woman who worked on the computer to expedite orders as they came in.

He assured me she was very good at her job, and she was the first one to notice the files had been eliminated. I told him that would make my interview of her even more valuable. We arranged for a time during the next week.

I then talked to Mark Whitlock. Yes, *talked* to Mark Whitlock. He called me. Somewhere in my probing I had tapped a person who knew where Mark was. My guess was that it was someone at his former law firm.

The conversation on the phone went something like this:

"Are you the guy they call Dataman?"

"I'm the guy they call lots of things, including Dataman, but I prefer Tom Walkinshaw."

"I understand, Mr. Walkinshaw, you've been trying to get in touch with me."

"I sure have. I just need to know if you're a blackmailer, kill people, or skip support payments to figure out why I want to get in touch with you."

He laughed. That seemed to eliminate killing and blackmailing. "I'm Mark Whitlock. I skip support payments."

"Your former wife doesn't like that. She plans to pay me a good chunk of money to find you."

"You won't find me."

He wasn't bragging, I could tell. In fact he seemed pretty casual about it, which gave me a sinking feeling I was going to be out some money. "I'm good," I said.

"And I'm a lawyer who's tracked a few people myself. I've pretty much learned the tricks of hiding. You won't find me unless I want to be found, and I don't want to be found."

"So why the call?"

"Curiosity. I want to know why Margorie is so interested in finding me."

"She says it's the money."

He laughed again. "I left her a substantial sum of money and she has a good job. Considering her claims, the loss of the money would be worth seeing me gone."

"You left her millions, then ..."

"Give me a break. I was a good lawyer, but not that good. She got three hundred grand from me, carefully invested to maximize a yearly return. I put the rest in a trust for my daughter, which Margorie doesn't know about, and can't touch when she does find out about it."

"I assume because you're in hiding the accusations she made were true."

I thought for a moment the line went dead. Then, from a deep silence, Mark Whitlock answered in a voice literally shaking with anger. "I want you to understand this: Not one word of what she said was true. *Not one word.* I absolutely love my daughter and I wouldn't do anything to hurt her."

"So why are you hiding?"

"Think about it. You're a respected lawyer in a good law firm. Your wife sues for divorce and then produces, privately between you and her lawyer, a psychologist's report that says your daughter has been molested and all signs point to you. She says she will not make this information public if you agree to a divorce, a large financial settlement, and custody of your daughter. Your option is to contest the divorce, in which case she'll launch a public battle for the custody of your child and turn over all reports to the police."

"I agree it's not something I'd want to happen to me."

"Me, either, only it did. And I didn't have too many options. I could have fought the divorce and the charges, but no matter what, my reputation as a lawyer and the good name of my law firm would have been irreversibly damaged. I had the report and the psychologist to deal with, and I was told outright that my daughter would testify against me."

"You still haven't explained why you ran."

"I didn't run. I walked away from a no-win situation. See, I know I didn't molest my daughter; therefore, I know I'm being extorted. Since I wasn't allowed to see my daughter anyway, I decided to save some of my dignity and take my firm out of harm's way. I divested myself of the assets I had left and moved on, cutting my losses. If I need something to give me a lift, I think of how angry Margorie must be at the end of each month when she doesn't get a check. She didn't need the money, but getting a check was like twisting the knife one more time."

"And what are you doing now?"

"That's just the kind of question I might ask if I was trying to trick someone into giving away his location. No harm, though, in the telling. I used to do a little gourmet cooking as a hobby. Now I'm working as a cook in a restaurant—this week. Next week no telling what I might be doing, or where I might be doing it."

"The toughest guy to catch is the one who keeps moving."

"Exactly."

"In a few days, I'd like you to call me. If you think I might be setting a trap, have someone I don't know call for you. I think I might have some information you'd like to have."

"So you're telling me you believe everything I say and you want to help me out of the kindness of your heart?"

"No, I'm telling you I believe Margorie less than you, and if I'm able to help you in any way, I expect you to pay the bill Margorie is sure not to pay."

Another long silence. "Okay." The line went dead.

Was I playing both ends against the middle? I didn't know yet. Not all the pieces were in place. I needed to know more about Denise Britt; I still needed to know more about Mark Whitlock. After that, I'd do the only thing I could that would get to the truth for me: I'd confront Margorie with the information I had and see what she said.

TWENTY-FOUR

They parked the van in the same parking lot where the killer had parked only a few months before. They parked at the far end where a large tree created deep shadows, and under a light that one of them had broken out the night before.

They came out of the van like a combat team, each of the five of them armed, three with handguns, one with a sawed-off shotgun, and the last, the leader, with an Uzi—the fact *he* had the Uzi was part of the reason he was the leader.

They wore dark clothes and black ski masks. Besides their weapons, they carried army surplus back packs. They moved along the shadows of the field, one at point, making sure the way was clear, another at the rear. They'd seen a lot of war movies together so they knew how to do this, and Juan Carlos—the one was the Uzi—had spent four months in the Marines before they threw him out.

They'd come to make a memorial for the two members of their gang who'd been killed here at Fremont High, by creating an incredible display of graffiti on the building as a tribute.

They weren't stupid; they knew how their friends died, and were determined it wouldn't happen to them. They came prepared: Two of them would do the painting while the other three set up a defensive perimeter. No one would get close to them.

Juan Carlos had suggested that maybe the killer would come for them, and the killer would be the one who got killed. That would make them heroes, which would avenge the deaths of their friends. The other four were not interested in the killer showing up. Deep in his heart, Juan Carlos didn't want him to show up, either.

Paco and Israel took the back packs and went to work on one wall of the building.

Manuel, the smallest and most agile of the group, climbed up a small fir tree next to the building; he was almost to the top when he thought he was high enough. He worked his body back and forth on the branch where he stood until the top of the young tree began to sway. When it swayed as close to the building as possible, he jumped and landed on the roof. He quickly scrambled along the edge of the building, reaching down to break out the floodlights that hung over the side every fifteen feet. He knocked out the lights on the side of the building they planned to paint, it being the only one they could defend from an intruder. Manuel then ran back to the tree, and, without a pause, leaped from the roof and crashed into its branches. He slipped down a few feet before he got a grip, and then finished his climb to the bottom to take up a defensive position.

Paco, with great skill, painted a Mexican flag flying at half-mast on a flag pole. Nearby, Israel, without the technical skill, but with a raw artistic talent, painted an eagle flying near the flag pole, with tears dripping from his eyes. They were quick and experienced, but these were large drawings and it took time to fill in the detail.

On the next space down, on each side of a bank of windows, the two began portraits of their friends who had been shot. They'd practiced these portraits over and over again because they wanted to make sure whoever saw them would recognize the pictures as those of their friends. They worked more slowly on these to perfect them.

Juan Carlos had taken up a position about forty feet away, near the soccer field. He snuggled in a slight depression in the ground beneath a tree in a very dark section of the field. There was enough illumination from the lights they'd left untouched, and from street lights in the distance for him to have a clear view of the field. If anyone tried to approach that way, he'd see him and kill him.

Frederico and Manuel took up positions near the access road that ran between the side of the school and soccer field, one at each corner of the building. From their positions they could see the front and back parking lots, which were still illuminated. Between the three guards, they could see someone coming long before that person could get close enough to harm them. They felt secure.

It took nearly a half an hour to finish the portraits. Juan Carlos was a little nervous about the time, but he'd chosen three in the morning because he knew few people would be awake then, and he knew it gave them about two hours before they had to clear out. The first janitor arrived at the school at five.

He took great pride in his planning. He knew the janitor would arrive through the back entrance to the school, and wouldn't pass the side of the building at all. In fact, it wouldn't be until the first students arrived before anyone noticed the drawings. If they'd tagged the front or the back of the building, it would've been noticed right away, and the janitors might have gone to work removing the work before the students arrived to see the masterpiece.

They would paint their gang signs on the last section of

the wall. They didn't care if anyone knew it was them—proving it would be another story. Juan Carlos was making a statement here: You didn't mess with members of his gang.

Another tree separated Israel from Paco as they worked on the gang graffiti. Both were feeling pretty proud of what they'd done; only Paco was a little nervous because his art teacher had admired a sketch he'd made that resembled one of his drawings. He was sure she'd know he was the one who'd done the painting on the side of the building.

While Paco worried, Israel died. He never saw the barrel of the gun tilt over the top of the building and take aim at the crown of his head. The power of the impact literally drove him to the ground. He was at one moment painting, and next he was a body on the ground, his face gone, unrecognizable. His friends never heard the shot that killed him.

A few seconds later Paco died. The barrel of the gun simply tilted to the left and fired.

Although Frederico didn't hear the shot, he felt something strange; something had brushed past his pants leg. He turned slightly and looked down, then reached down and touched his pants. His fingers came away dripping blood. He followed, with his eyes, a swath of spray on the ground that led back from his pants to Paco's body. He opened his mouth to scream a warning when the next slug smashed into his face, slammed him backward and sent his gun flying from his hand across the asphalt.

Juan Carlos heard the noise and it pissed him off. He'd warned them all that any noise carried into the night. He rolled on his back and lifted his head to see if he could find out who'd disobeyed him.

Manuel still stood on guard, to his left, peering around the corner of the building toward the front parking lot. He couldn't see anyone to his right. Frederico must have stepped around the corner of the building, but the other two should have been along the wall someplace. He squinted hard in the dark but couldn't see them.

He slipped over on his stomach and began to crawl closer to the building, the Uzi cradled across his arms. When he looked back to his left, he saw Manuel flat on the ground, too. Juan Carlos thought he must have seen something to make him drop. He was wrong. Manuel would never see anything again.

Juan Carlos stayed low and in the shadows. He kept trees and low shrubs between himself and the school, just in case. He worked his way down the field, closer to where the taggers should be. Tired of crawling, he crouched low, ran a dozen steps and then dove to the ground. Out of the corner of his eye he saw a tiny, pinpoint flash and then the soil near his feet erupted in a spray. He didn't wait to examine the small crater made by the slug; he simply ran as fast as he could and slammed his back against the building. He swept the sight of the Uzi back and forth along the edge of the roof. He didn't have to be told what had happened—he'd leaped over the body of Paco to get to the wall.

He saw a slight movement above and sprayed the spot with bullets. A few seconds later more movement came from farther down the building. He fired again. Right now, for the first time in his life, he wanted cops, and lots of them. He hoped everyone in the neighborhood had called 911 by now.

He inched down the building to the tree and hugged the shadows. He still scanned the roof line, moving the gun barrel back and forth along it. With any luck, he'd scared the man away.

From where he was he could see all four bodies of his

friends. It was clear now, because he hadn't moved, that Manuel was dead, too. The sight angered him. The killer had made a fool of him, Juan Carlos. He'd made all these careful plans, but he never thought to cover the roof. Why should he? How would the guy get up there? Only a Manuel had the quickness to get up there without a ladder.

Juan Carlos swept his head back and forth again. He was feeling a little better now because nothing had happened in a while, and in the distance he could hear a siren.

Off to his left, he heard someone shout, "Hey."

He looked in that direction and saw a man standing at the edge of the building. He had a rifle to his shoulder, pointed at Juan Carlos.

Juan Carlos whirled around and dove to the ground at the same time. Unfortunately the shooter had seen all of his moves from the roof top. He fired one shot and Juan Carlos was dead when he reached the ground.

The man turned back around the corner and followed the outline of the building, staying in the shadows. Up ahead of him a police car hurried into the parking lot with lights flashing and siren just dying out. The car swung in an arch through the parking lot, its headlights sweeping across the shooter.

The police car skidded to a halt, tires squealing; the doors were thrown open and the two police officers dived out. The one nearest the building took a slug in the side of his chest, part of it caught by the bullet-proof vest, part of it fragmented into him. He staggered along the side of the car toward the back, paused, and then slowly sank to the ground.

The other officer reached inside the vehicle and pulled out his shotgun, rose up over the top of the car and pumped out several shots in the the perp's direction.

The shooter was already fifteen yards from the spot. He

aimed his rifle quickly and fired. The bullet smashed through the back window of the police car, crossed through it, and caught the cop in his vest, stomach high. The impact tossed him backward, sending the shotgun pirouetting through the air, stretching him out on his back behind the car, the wind completely knocked out of him.

As he struggled to catch his breath, a rifle barrel appeared next to his head. He followed the barrel up to a face that smiled back at him. He tried to smile, too, just before the gun went off.

TWENTY-FIVE

We had one of those days in Oregon that you learn to live for. The weatherman had predicted clouds that would move in and we would see rain again. Instead high pressure unexpectedly shifted from the south, and with it came clear skies and warmer-than-forecasted temperatures.

We spent a good part of the day simply walking around the city. First we went up to Powell's for coffee and rolls, and a cruise through some of our favorite book sections, which in my case is anything having to do with islands, books or magazines.

When I came into the coffee shop carrying another book about St. Barts, Diane simply rolled her eyes and put down a book she was looking through.

"What is it about you and islands?" she asked.

"I don't know," I said, "I'm still trying to figure out why no man is one."

She wrinkled her nose. "Cute. Tell me, how many islands have you been on?"

"Do you want me to stretch out on the floor while I talk to you, Doc? Am I going to get charged for this? Does a continent count as an island?"

"You've already been charged; you paid for breakfast. So answer my question."

"Although I've never been on an island, I've always imagined that island life would have a simplicity to it that would be appealing."

"I see I'm going to have to take you to Hawaii and debunk your theory."

"Small islands appeal to me, not large ones."

"I'll have to do some research on the fascination with islands and then add what I find to my list of peculiarities I've discovered about Tom Walkinshaw."

"Are we talking a secret file here?"

"We're talking a thick, secret file."

"Two can play at this. What are you reading?"

"I'm not reading it, I'm just looking through it."

"That sounds like avoidance if I've ever heard it. Let me see."

She held up a book titled *You and Your Office*. "I thought it had a snappy title."

"There's only you in your office. How many problems can you have with that? You don't have to schedule coffee breaks, or vacations time, or who works on the weekends. Diane, you don't even have an office. You work in a living room."

"So, you work in a courtroom."

"No, I work in the remains of a courtroom. I actually left the building behind. Besides, all that oak in my office is a lazy man decorating. I didn't have to think about paint. I didn't have to think about wallpaper. I didn't have to think about carpeting. I only had to think about what oak thing went where."

"You've created a masculine masterpiece that would make Perry Mason feel proud."

"And you'll have the first office featured in *Better Homes and Gardens*."

"Good, now that we've got our quota of insults done for the day, let's go take advantage of the sunshine."

Which is exactly what we did. We walked down to Waterfront Park and strolled along the flood wall until we reached the grassy knoll that ran down to the river. There we stretched out on the grass and soaked up the sun, talking occasionally or reading the books we bought. Our conversations consisted of little tidbits like "Hmmm. Most plants don't do well under florescent lights," or, "Did you know that St. Barts is French?"

When we tired of laziness, we walked upstream to River Place and had lunch at a sidewalk café, watching the activity of people strolling on the boardwalk, folks on the boats at the moorage below, and windsurfers and sailors on the river itself.

Later we walked back down the Willamette to Saturday Market, which of course doesn't run just on Saturday, and spent several hours touring the booths and looking at the homemade crafts, from jewelry to hats. Diane was a sucker for earrings. She couldn't pass one by untouched, and in many cases, unbought. I like hats. I picked up two hat racks when I bought the pieces from the courthouse and had on them nearly a dozen hats I'd purchased and never worn. I added one more to my collection.

We bought a couple of sandwiches at one of the booths and had them wrapped to take back to the apartment for dinner later. We strolled back, hand in hand, each feeling pretty content with the lazy day we'd shared. Unfortunately, we wouldn't have a lazy evening; Diane had to meet with clients, and I had to check out the print-outs on the students, and I had some projects to get ready for the next day.

I knew the moment I turned the corner in the office building and saw Wilson leaning against my door that I'd have to alter my plans. I hadn't heard from him since he called and announced that our police protection was canceled. When I told him I still felt there might be a threat to my life, he laughed and said to get elected mayor and then I could have all the police protection I wanted. For now, though, he needed the cops for his investigation.

"You really should call ahead, lieutenant," I said. "We're not easy to find on a Sunday, especially since our police protection was canceled."

He moved out of the way so I could unlock the door. "I did call ahead. No one answered. I showed up in hopes of finding your bullet-ridden body, but you don't have a lock easily picked so I couldn't get inside."

I didn't know if he was kidding or not. "I'm touched by your concern. Is there any reason I shouldn't be in one piece?"

"After last night, we're checking on anyone involved in this case."

I shut the door carefully behind me, waiting until the last second to glance at Diane. The expression on her face was just what I thought it would be. It said: We did it again. "We've kind of turned off the world for the day, lieutenant. What'd we miss?"

He helped himself to my recliner. "Wouldn't it be lovely to take a day off from the world. Well, while you were away, your shooter bumped off five spics and a cop."

"Latinos," I said, dumbly. "I think that's what they like to be called." I pushed my chair over to Diane, then I sat down on the edge of a table, feeling a little weak in the knees. "What happened?"

"Five gang buddies of the first two victims decided to leave a memorial for them at the high school. I've got to give them credit. This is some of the best artwork I've ever seen spray-painted on a wall. They got wasted while they worked."

"Why on earth would they take such a risk?" Diane asked.

"I guess they didn't think it was a risk. They came armed. In fact, one of them had an Uzi. Three of them appeared to be standing guard while the other two painted."

"And he picked them off from a distance with his high-powered rifle."

The lieutenant smiled, I guessed at my ignorance. "He shot them from close range from the roof of the building. They didn't set up a very good defensive perimeter."

"That's strange," I said. "That roof's pretty high. How'd he get up?"

"We found some boxes and a barrel stacked up on a dumpster back by the service entrance. He would've had to do some acrobatics, but he could've gotten up that way."

"And he killed five more boys?" Diane asked.

"And one cop." Wilson answered.

"How'd the cop come into it?" I asked.

"One of the kids managed to fire off some rounds with the Uzi. The neighbors heard it and called us. The first patrol car arrived just as the killer was leaving the scene. Two officers confronted him. One got killed; one's in critical condition in the hospital."

"What do you want from me?"

"Anything. We're afraid we might now have a mad dog unleashed. He's tried to kill you. He's shot two cops. He's neither being as cautious as he was, nor is he being as discriminate with his targets."

"I see your point," I said. "I know there's reason to worry, but I think there's some hope, too."

"You're an optimist."

"No. He's come full cycle. He's back to the high school. Something at the high school will give us the clue to find him. By the way, you should have something on those video cameras on the roof."

"Yeah, right, that Jap shit only works when nothing's happening."

"It went out again?"

"Yeah. It happened last time, too."

"Last time you had a foggy night. You thought the moisture might have gotten to it. There was no moisture last night."

"I'm not an electronic genius like some folks. It wasn't working last night."

"Don't you think it's as suspicious as hell, though? I'd like to get a look at it."

"Don't expect an invitation soon."

"It seems that Tom is the one who's given you some of your biggest clues in this case," Diane said. "It might be worth your time to let him look."

I smiled to myself. This is the woman who was glad I wasn't still wrapped up in the case.

"I do have one thing to show you," I said. I went to the computer with the security camera and brought up the clip of the man trying to get in the doors. Wilson moved behind me and looked over my shoulder.

"What's that suppose to be?" he asked.

"I can't claim it as a fact, but I'm sure you're looking at the shooter." I went on to explain about my visit to the school and the person I'd seen standing in the doorway.

"Can you get me a copy of that?"

"I can give you a copy, but I'm not sure it'll do you much good unless you have a program to run it. Send Curry over and I'll do for him what I can."

"Have you got anything else?"

I gathered together all the printouts I'd collected over the last two days. "I've been running some checks on staff and students at Fremont High. This is what the computer has given me. I don't have any access to juvenile records, so I'm pretty sure you can find more than I can. The adults are pretty clean. I went from last year's yearbook, so this doesn't have the freshman class or any new staff members added this year. You're welcome to the stuff."

He gathered up the papers. "Over the next few days we're going to be at the school interviewing anyone and everyone we can. Once we're finished, those folks are going to want to finish up their school year and get on with their lives. The last person any of them will want to see is you. In the meantime, I'd keep a good look-out when you go out, and I definitely wouldn't go out at night. We're throwing everything we have into this investigation now, and we don't have anything left over to baby-sit you."

As soon as he left, I said to Diane, "I've got to get hold of Curry."

"Why?"

"I want to look at that camera equipment."

It didn't work. What are you going to learn from it?"

"I'm going to find out why some sophisticated Japanese camera equipment which is guaranteed to work in a typhoon, suddenly, and conveniently, goes on the blink during two very crucial times."

"You don't think that is coincidence."

"I think we need to find out when the cameras went dead; I think we need to find out who has access to that equipment; and I think we need to see what's on the tape the cameras shot before they went dead."

"I think you need to talk to Curry."

"I think you're right."

She came over and hugged me. "Don't go back to the high school," she said.

I knew why, but I asked anyway. "Why?"

"The last time, when he saw you there, he tried to kill you."

I laughed. "Maybe I'll go back late at night when no one's around. As long as I don't take a can of paint, I'll be safe."

"That's not funny."

"I'm sorry," I said, hugging her tighter. "I'll talk to Curry and see if I can get him to do the things I think need to be done. Believe me, though, it's just a matter of time before they'll get this guy. In fact, I think they'll have him before he hurts anyone else."

TWENTY-SIX

If I had a jaundiced view of human nature, I might say that it took the death of a police officer before the public reacted to the killings that had taken place. After all, the police officer represented the best values of a community, while taggers represented a threat to order. Diane assured me that it was the multiple deaths that had brought the community to an uproar, not just the death of a cop.

Whatever it was, a story that had already gotten a significant amount of media attention now seemed to get it all. Hour-long news broadcasts devoted as much as forty minutes to the murders. No more three-minute stories on the death of a tagger.

The fact that Wilson had stopped by to see me Sunday night, now, three days later, seemed more a miracle than anything else. The few times I was actually able to get through to the police station, I couldn't get Wilson or Curry. And neither of them were returning my calls.

I could only follow the story on the news like the other good citizens. The police had rolled into Fremont High with the idea of interviewing all the students they could. That turned out to be easier than they thought it would, because parents simply refused to send their children to a school where eight people had died. They had few students to interview.

At the end of each school day, a spokesman for the police department would meet outside the high school's front doors and announce that the investigation was continuing, that they had discovered some interesting clues, and that they could not talk about them.

My guess was they hadn't found out a thing they hadn't known before. One cop, in frustration, admitted to a reporter that the killer had even taken the time to pick up his shell casings. As in the other shootings, he hadn't left a single clue behind.

For me, that was an incredible statement. How can you commit a crime without leaving a footprint, or a fiber, or a smudge of some kind? And how, in this day and age, could a criminal investigator not find one of these things?

I'm being unfair. I'd learned from Curry in the last investigation that the killer wore Nike running shoes. The soles had a common design and the shoes were very popular. From the way the footprints varied in consistency, the cops believed that the shoes were anywhere from one to three sizes too large for him, and the killer stuffed them with something to make them fit. He is a clever fellow.

They also believe he encases himself in some kind of a plastic running suit with elastic arm and leg band, wears a head covering and rubber gloves. His clothing means he doesn't drop hairs or clothing fibers. He always left the scene with whatever he brought with him. He is very good, and even in the middle of this latest crime, with one surviving witness, and police converging on the scene while he was still close by, the cops apparently knew no more about him than they did before. Yes, he is very good indeed.

I had more than enough work to keep me busy, and Diane seemed to be picking up clients every day. Without additional information, it was pointless for me to sit down at my computer and rehash things I'd already hashed. I still wanted to see the surveillance cameras. I had left that message for Curry.

I decided, finally, that if they wouldn't come to me, I would go to them. One Tuesday afternoon I hopped in my car and drove to the high school. I wasn't sure what I was expecting to find when I got there, but I didn't find as much as I thought I would. Few student cars were parked in the front parking lot and the side of the building where the shootings had taken place looked pretty much the same. The police had apparently finished up their investigation of the shooting scene and tidied up after themselves.

That didn't mean they were gone. I counted more than a dozen marked and unmarked police cars in the lot, and the CSU van was parked alongside the building.

Fortunately, all I could see were vehicles and not cops. I parked my car and got out to walk around a bit, spotting the cameras' locations. I'd been told that they had six on top of the building, but from the front lot I could only see two.

After several unchallenged minutes, I decided brazen was better than nothing at all. I walked into the building. I ran into a cop immediately, sitting on a bench near the front doors reading the sports section from the *Oregonian*. When he noticed me, he carefully folded up the paper and then slowly got up to ask me what I wanted.

I continued to go for brazen. I pulled one of my business cards out of my wallet and handed it to him, saying, "I'm here to see Detective Curry. He's expecting me." I wasn't even sure Curry was in the building.

The cop pointed around the corner and said, "Curry's in the main office."

I nodded my head and walked around the corner as the

cop went back to the sports page. Actually, I had no intention of stopping in the office. If I did, Curry would hurry me out the door as fast as he could. I walked purposefully by the office door and headed deeper into the building, sure I'd find something of interest if I could just get enough time to look.

I made it as far as the janitor's room, which seemed the best place to find access to the roof. I couldn't have been inside the room for more than five seconds when the door behind me flew open and a booming voice yelled, "Stop!"

Through the whole thing, I was tempted to say, "Be gentle," but I was just as sure such a plea would get me slammed around. As soon as I stopped and put my hands in the air, two cops grabbed me from behind and shoved me into the nearest wall. While one of them kept me pinned, the other searched me (without gentleness.) Two hands grasping a semi-automatic pistol came into view just to my left and stayed there, unwavering, with the gun pointed at my head. I did my best to cooperate.

I was half carried and half dragged to the front office with my hands cuffed behind me and the gun dancing in and out of my view. I was hurried into the front office and shoved in a chair. Curry moved into my view with a startled look on his face. Ms. Cray moved in behind him with a smirk on hers.

"Gee, Ms. Cray," I said, "now I know why your students don't cut classes. Try to sneak into the janitors' room for a smoke and see what happens."

"Walkinshaw, what are you doing here?" Curry asked.

"I came to see you."

"You were told I was in the front office."

"I must have heard it wrong. I thought he said the janitor's office."

"Uncuff him," he said. "He's electronically brilliant, but when it comes to following directions, he's mentally impaired."

I rubbed my wrists and checked the cuts on my hand and arm to make sure they were okay. I seemed to have survived intact, but just barely. "I'd hate to see these guys when they're being brutal," I said.

"You're lucky you didn't get shot," he said, taking me by an elbow and directing me out the door.

"Hey," I said, "I thought he said you were in the janitor's office."

"Yeah, right." He continued to direct me out the front doors and into the parking lot.

"Come on, Curry," I said. "Talk to me."

He stopped me in front of my car. "Cute car. Every cop in town will now have a description of it. If it shows up at a crime scene again, you'll be arrested and it'll be towed away."

"Sweet talking will get you no where with me."

"Now's not the time to be clever, Tom. This last shooting has turned this case explosive, from the top of the department down, from the community up. No one has time for your jokes, nor does anyone want to take time for you."

"I know things are serious," I said. "And, I know if you'd returned my calls, I wouldn't be here, but I have to know one thing."

"First of all, we've been told to return no calls. Period. Second, you're no longer involved in this case. Run along and play with your computers."

"Okay, okay," I said, "I'll go peacefully if you'll just answer the one question."

"Walkinshaw ..." he said, looking like he was about to explode.

"Just one."

"Just one, and then get the hell out of here before Wilson sees you. He'll see that you get locked up, I swear."

"Did you check the cameras?"

"Of course I checked the cameras."

"And the wiring?"

"I checked the wiring. I spent hours in the crawl space above the ceiling checking each lead from camera to computer."

"No splices?"

"Not a one."

"No electronic relays anywhere?"

"Not a one."

"No transmitter that could broadcast the cameras' images?"

"Nothing."

"What about the computer itself?"

"No hidden files. No unusual programs."

"Are you sure there isn't something buried in one of the other programs on the computer?"

"I'm positive. The computer is dedicated. Running the cameras is the only thing it does."

"Then why did the cameras shut down when they did?"

"They've had problems with them before. Nothing serious, but an occasional glitch. They've failed to record a few times before. And now you've had your *one* question. Leave before I have explaining to do."

I was so sure that the cameras would provide some valuable information I was stumped. "You checked each line from the cameras carefully?"

"I followed each line," he said, obviously getting frustrated. "It's hot up there. It wasn't much fun. The heating vents run overhead. Believe me. I know what I'm doing. Now leave!"

I did believe he knew what he was doing. I was sure if he said there was no hidden program on the computer, there wasn't one. And I was sure if he hadn't seen a splice in a camera line, he hadn't seen one. But I wasn't convinced. Curry was very clever, but so was the killer—maybe more clever than Curry. I still wanted to see the cameras for myself.

It wasn't going to happen today, though. "Please," I said to Curry. "If you find anything, let me know." I did drive away finally, and I could see by the look on Curry's face he was more than happy to see me go.

The next day I got a message from Curry, in a surprising way. A messenger dropped off a package addressed to me. In it was a video tape and a note, which read:

Sorry I had to treat you so roughly. The department is playing hardball now. You did not hear the following from me. The video cameras seem to be working now. As you'll see when you watch a copy of the surveillance tape, it worked up to a point. We're guessing one of the taggers somehow jerked the cable and caused it to short out, probably the one on the roof, who's on the recording.

No killer on tape. No shootings on tape. You'll see a brief scene and then the camera shorts out. As I said, I checked the computer that runs the cameras. I found no hidden files and no hidden programs. I can't find any way these cameras are somehow sending a signal to the killer which is what you're thinking, right?

Our interviews with other gang members said they knew nothing about the plans to tag the building. In order to insure their secrecy, Juan Carlos Riveres apparently told no one what his plans were. He simply sent out an order to the other four to meet him two blocks from the school at 3:30 in the morning. He picked two artists who'd shown him some things they'd drawn, to remember their friends.

We're back to believing the killer must have some kind of a view of the school from where he lives. We're fanning out in the neighborhood.

If you can think of anything, let me know.

***

I was sure the killer didn't live within sight of the school; that was one of the first things I checked out. And I still wanted to see the surveillance cameras.

It wasn't until I'd watched the tape the fifth time that I actually saw the gang members approaching the school. The video was a little grainy, probably from being copied one too many times, and the equipment was medium-priced, which gave medium-priced results. The gang members were nothing more than a dark spot in the distance that moved, sort of like shadows and light in a wind storm. It wasn't until the kid jumped from the tree to the roof that I knew the taggers were there.

I watched him move down the edge of the building and knock out the lights. He didn't seem to be concerned about the cameras, nor should he have been. He was wearing a ski mask. It would have been almost impossible to identify him from the video tape.

I didn't see any other tagger come up on the roof, and I didn't see the one kid go near the camera. Suddenly the image began to flicker and then it went to snow. How convenient for the shooter.

I don't believe in coincidence. Especially not when it comes to electronic gear: equipment like this doesn't work one minute and not the next, only to work fine again later. It either went screwy and stayed screwy, or it went out. I wanted to see the cameras. I was sure I could find a clue the police hadn't.

I called the police station one more time and left a message for Curry. I told him again that I needed to get on the roof.

By the time Diane got off work and we sat down to dinner, I knew I wasn't going to hear from Curry. I knew I wasn't going to get an invitation to get on the roof. I knew I would have to figure it out for myself.

I began to wonder if the cops would still have the sight secured by this weekend. I wondered if I, too, could climb the same tree as the kid and make the same kind of leap to the roof. I wondered: if I did that, would the killer show up? At the same time I was wondering these things, I was trying to carry on a normal conversation with Diane. I knew for sure that she'd be one unhappy lady if she knew what I was thinking.

I didn't want to worry her, but I wasn't a fool. I had no intention of donning camouflage clothing and sneaking around the school grounds at night. I thought I'd just drive over there on Saturday morning when Diane had clients and walk into the building. I'd have maybe ten minutes to look around before the cops got to me. With any luck, I could get to the roof before then. It seemed like a good plan, anyway.

TWENTY-SEVEN

The building housing Wade Stewart's clothing factory was on the north side of Burnside, one of a dozen nondescript warehouses that Portlanders ignore on a daily basis unless a truck unloading goods is blocking the street.

The name of the company was on a small sign over a single door that led into a short hallway. At the end of the hall were double doors that led into the production line. To the right was a sign next to a stairwell that said OFFICES UPSTAIRS.

Four offices stretched across the front of the building. At one end was the reception area with a secretary who handled telephone orders. In the second office was the computer and fax that handled electronic orders. In the third office was the bookkeeper. In the fourth office was Wade Stewart. The rest of the second floor was taken up with storage for finished products and raw materials. Like the rest of the building, the storage areas and the offices were old and simply maintained.

Wade had invested in nothing fancy here. On one side of his office was the men's room, on the other side of the secretary's office was the women's room. His staff members either ate at their desks or went downstairs to the lunch room. Each office had an ancient air-conditioning unit hanging out a window, rusted on the outside and peeling paint on the inside. I was sure that each one worked, as much as I was sure that each one created an incredible noise that the staff had long ago learned to ignore.

I joined Wade in the second office, the one with the computer I had already met before. Here he introduced me to Judy Spanada, the woman who tracked the e-mail and fax orders, the one who first received the blackmail note, and the one who was first to notice that files had been eliminated.

I guessed Judy to be in her mid-thirties. She might have been an attractive woman in the bloom of youth, but now she was a bit faded and a bit plump. She'd been with Wade for fourteen years. I learned from the information Wade sent over that she'd gotten a divorce in her late twenties and had custody of her three children. She'd married young and now her kids were all teens, expensive, and a handful. Dad had remarried and could only provide the minimum support for the kids because he now had a new family, with two stepchildren and two more of his own.

Not all of this appeared in Judy's employment files. I'd asked Wade to pencil down everything he knew about the three people who worked upstairs for him. At first he'd been reluctant, but I insisted. I told him I could crack this one only if I had his help.

Mary Beth Ariano, his receptionist, was the youngest of the three. She'd been working for Stewart for three years and had been disciplined twice for arriving late for work and for abusing sick time. Mary Beth probably wasn't long with the company. She was getting married in June, and both Wade *and* Mary Beth hoped Mary Beth wouldn't need this job afterward.

Aaron Hawley was the bookkeeper. He'd been with the company from the beginning, working first for Wade's father and now for Wade. He was nearing retirement age, but he hadn't shown any interest in retiring. As he told Wade, he lived a simple life and his work was at the center of it. Without the job, his life would be too simple.

I knew that to be only partly true. Aaron's life was simple now, mainly because he was a survivor and most of his closest friends were not. Aaron was gay; he'd lost two partners to AIDS, but hadn't tested HIV-positive, because he didn't "come out" until late in life, and by then he knew about AIDS and took precautions.

None of this was a secret. He was a spokesperson for the Portland homosexual community, often seen on the news or quoted in the newspaper. Wade's only comment about the man was that he was a damned fine bookkeeper.

I wasn't too interested in Aaron or Mary Beth, but I needed to check to make sure I hadn't missed a connection. Judy Spanada was a different story. I'd been interested in her from the time I heard about the second set of files being wiped out.

The trap I'd set in the computer was not fool-proof, by any means. Even a hacker could eventually find it and circumvent it if he knew what he was looking for. But no one, not even me, could have found it as quickly as the blackmailer would have had to find it in order to wipe out that second set of files. No one sabotaged the computer by way of the Internet. The job had been done at the keyboard. That meant either Judy had done it, or someone had been given access to Judy's computer to do the job himself. It took a little time, but eventually I figured out which of those two possibilities was the way it happened.

After we entered her office, Wade introduced me to Judy. "Judy, this is Tom Walkinshaw. He's here to look at your computer."

Judy pushed back a bit from her desk and smiled broadly.

"For once Mr. Stewart, there's nothing wrong with my computer. One of the others must have called for repair. I didn't."

"Mr. Walkinshaw is not a repairman," Wade said. The smile faded just a bit on Judy's face.

"If I could sit down here for just a minute," I said, pointing at her chair. The smile disappeared completely and she didn't get up.

"Mr. Walkinshaw needs the chair, Judy."

Reluctantly Judy gave up her seat. "What's this all about?" she asked.

Neither Wade nor I answered. I spent a few minutes confirming that my trap was still in place and had not been circumvented. I then went to the records the trap kept and filed down through the times the computer was used. Within seconds I knew pretty much all I needed to know. Beside me Judy's eyes were growing bigger with each new screen that flashed on the monitor.

She mumbled, "I've never seen any of that before."

"No, you haven't," I said. "It's something I've added."

She stared at me, her face blank. She still hadn't figured it out. "You've worked on my computer before?" she asked.

"In a way," I said. "By the way," I asked, "how is Ernie Sternberger?"

"Ernie Sternberger?"

"Yes, Ernie. He works at Radio Shack in town."

She staggered back a step. "How do you know Ernie?"

"I go to Radio Shack occasionally when I need the odd connector I can't get anywhere else."

She relaxed a bit, but now Wade was the one who tensed. He obviously picked up cues better than Judy. "What's going on here?" he asked.

This was the part I hated the most. When people asked me

to find out something for them, they didn't want the news to be bad. They especially didn't want to find out there was a bad guy in it, and that bad guy was someone they trusted. Wade was happy as long as his blackmailer was anonymous, some son-of-a-bitch he could denigrate without having to know him.

"What's going on," I said, "is Ernie down at Radio Shack has been dating Judy for a year or so. Using information she provided, he came up with a scheme to blackmail you."

Judy staggered back two more steps and suddenly sat down in the middle of the floor. She brought the back of a hand to her mouth as if she was trying to stifle her own scream. Nothing came out, but she turned pale and her eyes became huge.

"There must be a mistake," Wade said.

"No," I said. "No mistake. I really didn't need to look at the computer. That was for your benefit. I'd already logged-on and looked earlier, the same way I logged-on to the computer at the Radio Shack store and found Ernie's e-mail messages. I've downloaded those and saved them, so it won't do him much good now to try to take them off his computer, though I'm sure he'll try when he finds out what's happened here."

Wade slowly turned from me to Judy. "Judy?"

"He said we'd never get caught," she cried. "He said it was fool-proof."

"Not fool-proof," I said, "or I never would have caught you. On the day the second set of files disappeared, he e-mailed you in the morning to destroy those files. You stayed at your desk during the noon hour to eat your lunch. The others went down to the lunch room. You destroyed the files, and then, two hours later you told Mr. Stewart that the files had just been destroyed. I have a record of it all, recorded on the program I hid in the computer, including his e-mail message to you, and the original, which is still on the computer at Radio Shack."

Still crying, she said, "He said we could get married if we could just get a little money ahead."

"About fifty thousand ahead," I said.

Wade Stewart looked as stricken as Judy. I don't think he believed for a minute that this would turn out as it had. "I don't know what to say."

I did. Wade liked Judy. He always had. She, too, was loyal to Wade—to a point. The point was when desperation took hold. I could only guess, but I probably wouldn't be too wrong if I said that Judy was near panic. Her kids were growing up, one about to leave for the military, another getting ready to move to Seattle to take a job, and the third a senior in high school. She'd focused her life on these kids, and now they were going to be gone. Heading toward forty, she needed something in her life to replace them. Along came Ernie, one of not many to come along. The rest was electronic history.

"Let me say it for you: I'm going to sit down at this computer and send Ernie an e-mail message. Basically it's going to tell him to get out of town fast or face prosecution. Then you're going to work out a plan for Judy to pay you back for the money you'll need to pay me. After that, the two of you will have to have a long talk to see if you can still work together."

He reached down and helped Judy to her feet. She suddenly threw herself into his arms and began bawling, her head buried in his shoulder. He glanced at me, with a look on his face that said basically, get out.

I typed in the e-mail message to Ernie and sent it. I then put the computer back on line and got up to leave. Wade was leading Judy into his office as I shut the door behind me.

I felt old going down the stairs. Wade would pay me the money he owed me, and if he ran into someone with an information problem, he'd recommend me. But as of today,

I'd be the one who would be the target of his anger because I'd been the one to tilt his world. There was no good reason for it, but I knew he had to direct the anger someplace. He couldn't direct it at himself, after all, because he hadn't done anything. And he couldn't direct it at Judy for long, because if he did he couldn't keep her on, which I was sure he would do. So I was the one.

I walked back to my own building, smiling to myself as I walked. I was sure I could hear Ernie packing his bags and Judy begging for forgiveness. In the end everyone but Ernie would be better off. Wade would be back to have me make his system more secure. Once she had proven herself faithful again, Judy would have a better relationship with her boss than ever before.

Of course, Judy wouldn't have Ernie, and if someone else didn't come along, then she'd only have her work and her absent kids. I knew a little bit about that. I didn't wish it on her, and I thanked God one more time for Diane.

TWENTY-EIGHT

I gave myself all sorts of reasons why I shouldn't go back to Fremont High. Being arrested was at the top of my list. Being in danger was second. Making Diane mad was third. I tried to reason against these good arguments, pointing out that I needed more information, that I wasn't one to give up easily, and that I shouldn't be in any danger if I went during the day. Good sense should rule in such matters, but it didn't. I had to prove for myself the splice didn't exist.

When I drove into the parking lot at Fremont High, other cars were already there, and people were entering through the front doors. I was game. I parked my car and walked through the front doors, too.

Inside the doorway was a custodian who asked me if I was a parent there for information about the summer school session. Of course I was. He directed me to the library at the center of the building.

I had no intention of going to the library. I wanted to get on the roof; access had to be inside the building. I also knew that good planners wouldn't put it in a place that students could get to easily. I also knew that when I was in high school the one place students were told never to go was in the boiler room. Every high school had a boiler room.

At Fremont High School a boiler room by any other name was a Maintenance Room. When I found it, I discovered below the sign that identified it as the Maintenance Room another sign which said students were to stay out. And, of course, since this was not a school day, the room was unlocked.

I wasn't sure if this building had a boiler or not, but it did have five large tanks wrapped in insulation lined up in a row in the room, along with a lunch table for the custodians, huge stacks of cleaning supplies, and an assortment of ladders, so, if worse came to worst, I could run one of the longer ladders outside and get on the roof that way.

There were two other doors in the room. Behind one I found a storage room full of more supplies. Behind the second one, I found another storage room, only this one had special cabinets for inflammable liquids and semi-hazardous materials. Also, in one corner of the room was a steel ladder attached to the concrete block wall that disappeared into a shaft in the ceiling. The room was fourteen feet high. I estimated that the crawl space between the ceiling and the roof was another six feet.

I found a trap door at the top of the ladder that led to the roof. I also found a hinged panel that opened into the crawl space where a lot of the mechanisms of the building were wired and plumbed.

I went onto the roof first. Once I was up there, I found that the clue I'd expected to jump out at me, didn't. I examined the security cameras on all four corners of the building. Each one was mounted on a pole that shoved it about fifteen feet in the air. Two other cameras were mounted on taller poles in the center of the building and scanned the grounds farther away. A cable ran from the cameras and disappeared into a hole in the poles. Wisely, the cable was protected. Even if a student could have gotten on the roof, he would have had a tough time reaching the camera, and no luck reaching its cable. The pole was made of tempered steel and barbed wire had been spiraled around it from roof to camera and welded on. No one was going to monkey with these cameras, especially from the roof. So much for the police theory that one of the taggers had disabled the camera from here.

I climbed back through the hatch, expecting at any moment to hear a police siren. A red light on each camera showed that they were on, and one of them rotated in a 360° turn so that it could see the roof top. If the police didn't show up now, I'd probably hear from them on Monday after the tapes had been reviewed.

Of course, if there was no reason to review the tapes, I might not hear from them at all if nothing suspicious happened here this weekend. This was turning out to be easier than I thought it would be. That is, until I got in the crawl space.

Most of the building had suspended ceilings. Narrow walkways had been built over the top of the ceilings for maintenance purposes and ran between wooden trusses. As long as I stayed on the walkways, I could almost stand up straight. Fire walls were constructed between rooms and hallways, which meant to get around in the crawl space I had to open small doors to go from one area to the next. I got lost more than once.

I had a simple plan: locate the camera cable where it came through the roof and track it back to where it went through the ceiling into the main office. I wanted to make sure the cable hadn't been spliced into anywhere along the line.

But the cables made it untouched to a conjunction mounted below the roof. I discovered that an hour after I started, sweaty, dirty and discouraged. From the junction box, a single cable snaked its way toward the front-office computer. I followed its length and found nothing, just as Curry said.

The problem with finding nothing was that it didn't make sense. The killer had to have some way to know the taggers were at the school. The fact that the cameras conveniently went out during both shootings absolutely had to be connected.

I went back and started on the roof, tracking the cables one more time back to the junction box. Still nothing. I tracked the main line again. I probably never would've found a thing if I hadn't turned around to glance back at the line from a distance. The line came down a wall, disappeared behind a heating pipe, and reappeared below it. What caught my eye was the fact the line didn't go straight down behind the pipe; it had a slight bend in it, as if something was tugging at it behind the pipe. Up close you didn't notice the bend. A few feet away you did.

The pipe was made of flexible aluminum. I was able to crawl under it and pressure it away from the wall. There I found where the line had been severed and a T-joint inserted. The joint had been secured to the wall slightly off center from the line, as if it had been attached to the wall first and then the line cut and spliced into it. The third line, the one attached to the leg of the T, disappeared into the heating pipe.

I'd been out to prove that these cameras were not what had alerted the killer to the presence of the taggers. I hadn't really expected to find this splice which I was out to prove wasn't there. I stared at it, dumb-founded. I was much nearer to the killer.

I followed the pipe for some distance in both directions. I found what I was looking for finally, a ways from the office. More wires came down from the roof, disappeared behind the pipe, emerged at the bottom and went on down through the ceiling. The interesting thing about these wires was that one more came down from behind the pipe than came down from the roof. I got my bearings and then worked my way back to the ladder. Once again I went through the trap door on the roof, and found the wires coming out of the roof. They were attached to several pieces of equipment, from a wind gauge to a thermometer.

A local university offered a program to a number of schools from Portland, down the valley and throughout Oregon, which provided networked-computers and equipment, that gathered weather information. The information the schools compiled was invaluable. The university and the weather service had twenty-four hour weather information from over two dozen spots in Oregon, and the students got to work on practical projects.

I tried to imagine why someone, for any reason, would have connected the video feed to a weather computer. I couldn't think of anything, but I didn't work here. I'd call Ms. Cray on Monday; perhaps she'd know.

I had just latched the trap door to the roof when the lights went out in the tunnel. I thought maybe the meeting was over and the janitor had closed up the building, except I was pretty sure that had happened almost a half hour before. The last time I was on the roof, the only car I saw in the parking lot was mine.

I thought the janitor could still be in the building, but I didn't think he looked happy to be there when I came in, and I couldn't imagine him staying long after the others had left. Still, I didn't think the lights went out by themselves.

I heard the storage room door open ever so softly, down below. If I tried to open the trap door, I'd be caught in a flood of light. I decided to climb back into the crawl space. I moved down the walkway to the next door through the fire wall and paused to listen. I could hear someone climb the ladder.

After a long pause the trap door was thrown open with a

loud crash. I heard something scrape on metal and then another long silence. When I heard the trap door shut again, I figured that was my clue to go through the door in the firewall. I heard the door in the previous space open.

Hopefully the janitor had heard a noise and was investigating, or maybe he wondered why my car was still in the parking lot and was looking around. The one thought I was trying to avoid was the one that said the killer was about thirty feet away from me.

Whumppp! That's all it took to end avoidance. A hole about the size of my fist appeared through the door not more than eight inches from my head. I set a world record in walkway running, making it through the next door just as another hole appeared.

Oh, how I wanted to peek through that hole to see who it was with the gun! Right now I had to guess that it was one of four science teachers in the building, although one of them was a woman and an unlikely suspect. It could be one of the remaining three, but then, it still could be a student. A clever science student could be a clever killer. I'd narrowed the suspects from most of a city to maybe a dozen people. I hoped I lived long enough to pat myself on the back.

I put as much space and as many doors between myself and the killer as I could. Up here his scopes wouldn't do him much good unless we both ended up in the same space at the same time, which would make me dead.

I kept trying to tell myself that I had an advantage. The territory was fresh in my mind. He'd probably only been up once to splice the cable. As I kept moving, I couldn't keep my head from working on two problems at once: the cable and staying alive. Moving was going to keep me alive. The cable didn't get quite as much attention.

My thoughts were brief as they flashed by: To be networked, the computer must have a modem. Video images from camera fed to computer. If someone could access the computer remotely, they could pick up the video feed from the cameras; the killer could see what the camera saw in the comfort of his home. When it saw a tagger, the killer simply grabbed his gun and went out for a kill. He must live fairly close by. How could the computer have a video feed without a teacher knowing about it?

No more time. I was halfway through a firewall door when the next shot nearly took off my head, but it took off the top corner of the door instead. I quit trying to keep track of where I was. I started moving through doors as fast as I could, not even bothering to close them behind me. I needed distance.

What seemed like a good tactic at first looked like pure disaster when I found myself in a huge area, in the center of which was a large air-conditioning/heat exchange unit. From being on the roof, I knew that there were eight of these; this one was probably over the cafeteria area.

The walkway moved right to it, and then around it to continue out on the other side. I had just scrambled around it when I heard the shooter come through the doorway.

I would never make it to the next door.

I looked around frantically for anything that might give me a chance. In front of me was a grill that led into duct. I took a quarter out of my pocket and used it as a screw driver to loosen the clasps that held a light-weight aluminum grill in place. I quickly leaned around the corner and threw it like a Frisbee in the direction of the killer.

Damned if I didn't hit something. I heard a cry of pain and the sound of the rifle clattering onto the ceiling panels. I peeked around the corner, and though I couldn't see much, I could just make out the shadowy figure of a man stretched out, apparently trying to reach the rifle that he'd dropped. I didn't do two things: I didn't rush the man, like a good hero should. I knew he could and would kill me; I didn't even know if *I* could even seriously hurt another person, even in self-defense. And I didn't stick around to see if he was going to reach the rifle. I dove into the duct. Wedging my body into it, I was able to work my way up to the roof. At the top of this tunnel was a cap that was slotted underneath to allow fresh air to enter the system. I pushed myself right up against the cap and then bent my head and heaved my shoulders into it. The cap went flying off. I scrambled out of the tunnel and onto the roof.

It took a few seconds to figure out where I was. I moved toward the trap door, figuring I could get back down the ladder and out of the building before the killer. I was wrong. I was still thirty feet away from the hatch when it suddenly flew open.

I turned to my right, ran as fast as I could, and leaped off the side of the building, landing high up in a fir tree. I held on tight and broke my fall, although the tree swayed back and forth in a frightening way. The branch I held onto snapped and sagged just as another bullet blew off the top of the tree. I let go, falling through the tree, grabbing a branch just long enough to slow my fall before letting go again. Another bullet ripped through the tree and exploded near where my feet hit the ground running. I shot off around the corner of the building and kept going toward of my car. Apparently, the killer wasn't as good shooting moving targets as ones standing still. A small crater appeared in the asphalt ahead of me. My senses were super sharp. Someone expecting a bullet in the head tries to hear it before it gets there. At least I did. I wanted to know if I was going to die.

I didn't hear the bullet. I heard the bolt on the rifle work another shell into the chamber. I heard the silence that gave me hope I could dive behind my car before the next shot, and I heard the trigger being pulled, which meant I *wasn't* going to make it in time.

And I heard the click that said the killer was out of bullets.

I stayed behind my car for only a minute. I knew this guy was capable of coming off the building to get a shot at me from another direction. I popped my head up. He wasn't anywhere in sight. I slipped into the driver's side of my car, keeping as low as I could. The car started on the first try and left a long patch of rubber shrieking out of the parking lot.

I stopped at the first phone booth I saw and call the police, screaming at them to get to the school, and get Curry to meet me at my office. I wanted to get back to my computers as fast as I could; if I could tap into the science computer, I might be able to trace it to the killer's home, before he could disable it from the science room.

Of course I couldn't find a parking space close to my office, so I had to put the Healey back in the garage. I was out of breath by the time I got inside. I sat down at my most powerful computer and went to work. I went straight to the weather service's local web site. It didn't take much to break into its link to the university. Once there, I logged-on to Fremont's computer. I was on a roll, for a minute anyway—I got the weather; I couldn't find a video link.

I was sure he couldn't have had time to destroy it. The hardware alone would take time to unhook. I guessed he had the whole setup buried in a secret file, either to hide it from the teacher or the students. A quick check of the drive showed that there were some hidden files. A little more playing said I needed a password to get in.

I could have spent the rest of my life trying to guess the password. I didn't bother. This wasn't the Pentagon—I broke into the password protection program. I didn't waste time trying to find the password coded in the program. I rewrote part of the program, basically telling it to ignore all previous passwords and to use my new one. I found the video. This wasn't going to be as easy as I thought it would.

He'd installed a video card in the computer that converted the video signal to a computer signal and then back again. That meant he could see the video from the camera on his own monitor, or he could send it via modem to another computer or even to a television monitor. He'd written the secret files to use the modem without anyone detecting it.

I had to go back in and try to break into some more protection programs. Each one was a little more complicated than the next. He didn't seem to care if someone eventually found that he could hook up to the security camera, but he did care if they found out he could send out the signal through the modem.

I kept at it for nearly forty-five minutes. Just when I thought I was getting close, suddenly my screen blanked out, and then it began flashing red. A few seconds later, a message scrolled down the screen, one word at a time:

You're
    dead,
        Dataman.

That was the end of my hunt: He was back at his computer, destroying the link so it couldn't be traced.

Just then Diane walked into the office. She asked, with her usual cheerful voice, "Did you have a quiet morning?"

TWENTY-NINE

Diane didn't speak to me after she found out what I'd done. It didn't help to have an office full of cops, either. In the middle of it all, she announced that she was leaving, since this didn't have anything to do with her, only the idiot over there, referring to me.

The cops weren't happy with me, either. They complained because I'd left the scene. I made it clear that I wasn't going back over there until they had the killer in jail. I was pretty sure now, I said, that he didn't like me.

Curry showed up late in the afternoon, after I'd given my statement at least thirty-five times. He was certainly a lot more cheerful than the others. He sent most of them away, keeping one outside in the hall. He'd seen the last message from the killer, since it was still on the computer screen.

When we were alone, he said, "I thought sending you that video tape would make something happen."

"Thanks a lot. I know people who served in Viet Nam who were shot at less than I have been."

"Your theory turned out right, though; there was a connection between the video cameras and the killer."

"You should be pretty close to making an arrest," I said.

He laughed. "Hold that thought."

"You know it has to be one of the science teachers. A stretch might make it one of the hot-shot science students."

"Hold on, hold on," he said, stopping me. "I've just spent several hours in the high school, crawling through the ceiling just like you, and checking out the other computers in the building. Let me tell you, that building has a lot of computers."

"And you didn't find any others linked to the cameras."

"Not a one."

"Which means it's someone in the science department."

"Which means it's someone who has access to the building."

"Come on. Get real. It's got to be someone in the science department."

"This may come as a surprise to you, but the science computer is the only one in the building with its own modem. The rest of the computers are networked through the district office. That's where the servers are located. So, if you want to cruise the Net at Freemont, you network through a modem in the district office."

"The only way the killer could avoid going through the district with the camera feed was through the modem in the science department. The server at the district automatically logs any signals going through it. The killer wouldn't want that, a written record. So he used the computer in the science lab."

"And how would he get access if he wasn't in the science department?"

"One classroom key opens all the classrooms in the building. Any teacher could get in. Any custodian. Anyone could get in who had one of two sets of lost keys from this year. The building's scheduled to be re-keyed this summer."

I wasn't ready to give up, but I could see I wasn't going to push Curry into action. I tried anyway. "I'd get a search warrant for the homes of the science teachers. If you don't do it now, and one of them is the killer, I bet by the time you get one, you won't find a scrap of evidence."

"It always amazes me how civilians want cops to violate citizens' rights as long as it's not theirs. I don't have enough just cause to get a search warrant."

"You'd find just cause if he'd tried to kill you twice, and he'd promised to do it right next time."

"So, you'll have around-the-clock police protection again, until he's caught."

"A cop outside my door?"

"Unless the two of you want to make room for him in your bed."

"As mad as Diane is, I don't think there'll be the two of us in my bed."

"I can't blame her. It was a dumb move on your part."

"You wouldn't let me look at the cameras."

"It wasn't my call to make."

"Well, tell whoever's call it was to make, I was right."

"I'm sure he knows already. I certainly do. I was wrong about the splice."

I nodded my head. It wouldn't do me much good to keep saying "I told you so." "What's next?"

"We find the killer."

"And how are you going to do that?"

"The good old-fashioned way. With police work. We're dusting the cable and splicer for fingerprints. We're even trying to get fingerprints off the video board, although that's not going to make anyone happy. Once we get powder on the board, it'll be ruined. We'll try to trace the board and see who bought it. Eventually we'll find something to lead us to the killer."

"What's to keep him from killing in the meantime?"

"If you're right, he's getting rid of evidence at this moment, including the rifle. He won't have a weapon to kill with."

"What makes you think he doesn't have other weapons?"

Curry sat down at my computer and erased the death threat from the screen. He'd already saved it to disk. "The weapon he's using is at least twenty years old. The cop who lived is talking now. He doesn't remember much about the killer himself, but he remembers seeing the gun when the guy walked by to shoot his partner. He said it was huge, a hunting rifle like you'd see in those old jungle movies. It had a scope on it, and attached to the end of the barrel was a Campbell's soup can full of holes."

"Old means it's probably unregistered."

"Right."

"So why doesn't he have another gun?"

"He might, but my guess is he'd get rid of whatever he has so he will be squeaky clean when we get to him. He knows we're coming. No matter how clever he is, he's left too many clues behind by now."

"Let me ask you this," I said. "If you're so sure he'll be unarmed, are you willing to go into his house with your gun in your holster?"

"Yeah, right." He got up. "Listen, leave the rest of this to us. You've given us the leads we need. We'll get him now. You're a hero. Leave it at that."

"You could be allowing him time to get away."

"You want to get him today; we'll have him by next weekend. Just be patient. And by the way, we've kept the press out of this last shooting. You're the only witness. I thought you'd appreciate it if I kept them from hounding you."

"Thanks."

I gave him a couple of minutes to get out of the building,

smiled nicely at the cop in the hall without inviting him into my office and immediately got on the phone.

I called Beth Armstrong, the only teacher at the school who had contacted me.

She was still home, she explained, but just barely. She and her husband were leaving for Europe for a two-week vacation. God, she needed it, she said. The last week at the school was a nightmare. Many kids were in shock, or grieving for the dead teens. A few, though, let it be known smuggly that the kids had it coming to them, which created a great deal of racial tension. It didn't help to have police pouring over the building, stirring everything up.

I listened patiently. Obviously she needed someone to talk to about this, someone to unload on all the grief she felt herself. Finally, when she began to die down, I asked my questions.

"Beth, I called to find out about your science department at the high school. The police found some things there that interested them that maybe only the science teachers could explain."

"There's not much to tell about them," she said. "Mary Ann had her last day on Friday, of course. She has her administrative certificate, and she's got a job as a vice principal in a school down south. We were all so excited for her. Ken's been hauling the tennis team all over the state to tournaments, and then he did his five-day biology field trip at the last minute, which threw everyone's testing schedules off. He and twelve kids were at the coast for those days. Fortunately, he was gone when the boys got killed. Larry's still on crutches. He had that knee operation in April and still has trouble walking. Irwin's the only one who hasn't had his life turned upside down."

"Irwin?"

"Irwin Syzmoore. If you've ever heard of anyone being called too conservative for his own good, that's Irwin."

"I know something about the others," I said, "but I don't know much about Irwin. Tell me more."

"He's been teaching here forever, but nobody really knows him because he's so quiet. I know he belongs to one of those conservative churches, one you don't hear a lot about."

"How does he get along with students?"

"He's not much of a disciplinarian. They give him a bad time, but nothing malicious. I think the students don't know what to make of him."

"Does he get along with staff?"

"As long as you don't talk politics. The only time I ever see a reaction from him is when some highly liberal view is expressed. He's definitely conservative."

"He must be one of Ms. Cray's favorites."

"Hardly." Her voice dropped as if she was about to share a secret with me. "Rumor has it she's put him on a plan of assistance."

"What's that?"

"She's identified some problems in his classroom. She set up a plan of action to correct the problems."

"And if the problems don't get corrected?"

"He could lose his job."

"And what kind of problems are we talking about?"

"As I said, he's not very good with discipline. His room is always messier than the others at the end of the day, and he's had a problem with students carving gang signs on his desk tops."

"How's he handling all of this?"

"He's so quiet it's hard to tell. I suppose he takes it out on his wife."

"His wife?"

"They're such a cute couple; he can't be more than five five himself, and she can't be more than five foot."

"Did you know she's filed for a divorce?"

She gasped. "Impossible. She's devoted to him."

"I ran across it in some records I was going through."

"That is a stunner. He really has had a stressful spring, hasn't he?"

"You don't know the half of it," I said. I thanked her for her time, wished her a good vacation, and hung up.

I wondered how long it would take for Curry or Wilson to work their way back to Irwin. A woman looking forward to a new job, a man on crutches, and another man out of town, aren't going to be out killing people. I'd call the cops now, but I was sure they'd say "thank you for the information," but they'd continue to do it their way. After all, a hundred other people who might have had access to the computer could have reasons for going over the edge, too, but how many of them would be short enough that a rifle in their hands would look huge?

Okay, I'd play the game their way. They wanted proof. I'd give them time to find proof. Besides I had one more unpleasant task to do involving Margorie Whitlock. Once that was done, though, I'd be paying close attention to the progress the police were making. If it wasn't enough, I had one more thing I could do to see if I was right.

THIRTY

If some people thought that a man lacking both personality and sharp intelligence should consider a career in a uniform, they would have loved the police officer assigned to me as a body guard. The extent of our conversation after four hours together was whether or not it was appropriate for him to give me a lift in his patrol car to River Place.

He decided that since the trip was more official for me than for him, he didn't feel right allowing me to ride in the car. He preferred to follow me while I drove my car. I tried to explain to him that it wasn't worth my effort to get my car out of the parking garage to make such a short trip, which he didn't quite grasp, being a native Oregonian who feels that the driving of a car is a necessity and a right, which also explains why mass transit's slow to take hold in this state.

So I walked. He followed along in his patrol car, generally disrupting traffic because of his slow pace and specifically making an issue of his authority by flashing his lights and once blipping his siren to move people out of his way.

He followed me on foot right up to Margorie Whitlock's apartment and took up a position outside her door when the maid let me in. I was shown into the living room and left standing for nearly half an hour before Ms. Whitlock appeared.

People who keep you waiting send out all kinds of messages; the primary one being that their time is more important than your time; i.e., they're more important than you. People who keep you waiting for an extended period of time send out the same message, only they're determined you get it.

I've no idea why Margorie found it necessary to send such a message to me; maybe this was a message she was sending out to all men since her divorce.

When she finally came in, she said simply, "Sorry to keep you waiting. I was busy."

To make sure my judgment of Margorie isn't totally biased, I need to explain that she doesn't work anymore. She has a maid to take care of the heavy-duty chores. She's kept a low profile since her husband left, which means she hasn't been involved in many activities other than staying fit at the club and staying buffed at the beauty shop.

I suppose she could have been busy with child care, except her daughter was enrolled at a private boarding school in Portland and lived on campus, not with her mother. Needless to say, I had trouble finding an excuse for her that explained why she was so busy she couldn't walk thirty feet to tell me, or ten feet to tell the maid to tell me how busy she was going to be.

For balance, I should say something nice about her. Unfortunately, I had nothing nice to say. She gestured for me to sit while she took up her favorite position at the window with one hand clutching the curtains.

As I sat, I said, "I wish I'd known you were going to take a while; I could have told the policeman outside your door to take a break."

That brought her head around in a hurry with just the right amount of satisfying worry written on her features. "Police?"

"Police," I said, and left it at that. "I think I can bring some closure to this case."

"You found my husband." I expected some reaction from her, but her face remained fixed, the worry still a hint there, but certainly nothing else. No joy. No anger.

"I'd be more accurate to say that he found me. I got a call from him a few days ago."

"And he told you where he was?"

"That's the bad news. He hasn't told me where he is, and he's made it pretty clear that he plans to do whatever he must to keep me from finding him."

Her fingers tightened on the curtain. "Such as?"

"He plans to keep moving, keep changing jobs; I suspect he'll even change identities with each move."

"But you can still find him?"

I smiled. "Smart, well-educated men like your former husband who don't want to be found more than likely won't be found. He knows enough not to make the kind of mistake that will get him found, and as best I can tell he trusts only one of the people I talked to, and I honestly can't tell which one it is."

"You promised me you'd find him." Her voice was flat, the accusation without much force.

"No," I said, "I said I wouldn't charge you if I didn't find him, but I thought I could. Now I know I can't, and I have no intention of charging you."

She turned away and started out of the room, saying to me, "Then we have nothing more to talk about."

"There is one thing," I said, failing with this to slow her stride., "but I think you might want your neighbor to hear this, too."

She managed three more strides before she stopped and then did the slowest turn I have ever seen. When she could trust herself to speak, she said, "Neighbor?"

"Yes, your neighbor, Denise Britt. You must be very good friends. I see you bought her condominium for her."

She swayed ever so slightly on her feet and turned quite pale. She let the words slide out on a single breath. "She's at work."

"You'll just have to relay the information, then."

"The information?"

"I pieced it together," I said. "Mark might have figured it out, too, if he'd had one key fact."

"About my daughter?" she asked dumbly.

"About your uncle."

She dropped from her knees into a swoon and fell to the carpet before I could get to her. I called for the maid before I touched her. I didn't want any accusations about my behavior after all of this was over. With the maid's help, I carried her to the sofa. The maid returned with a wet cloth for Margorie's head, but with nothing in the way of sympathy apparent.

"She fainted when I gave her some bad news," I said.

The maid stared down. "I'm sure she has her fair share of things to faint about," she said, and then walked out of the room.

I sat in an armchair and waited patiently for Margorie to come around. It didn't take long for her to stir, and then within a minute or so her eyes darted open and she gasped when she saw me.

"You've had a bit of a shock," I said. Since I had a captive audience and since she no longer had far she could fall, I decided to hit her with it all. "I'm not sure why you never told Mark about your rich uncle. I don't know if you wanted to surprise him some day, or if you planned all along to dump Mark when you knew you were going to inherit the seven million dollars. I don't think you really knew for sure yourself what you were going to do until you were forced into it after your uncle died suddenly of a stroke."

She turned her face away from me and closed her eyes. She seemed to be trying to will me away, to will me to be quiet.

Perhaps she was even plotting how she might make me be quiet. I wasn't too concerned, because I was sure that Denise Britt was the strength here, not Margorie.

I continued, "You'd already started your affair with Denise nearly a year earlier after you met her at the athletic club. The plot to divorce Mark and keep custody of your daughter was hatched long before your uncle died.

"Mark wasn't interested in a divorce, though. He was one of those new, modern men who wanted to try counseling and reconciliation. That didn't fit into your plans of a large settlement for both child and spousal support, the settlement you thought you could get if you could blackmail Mark with an accusation of child abuse. Of course he knew nothing of your relationship with Denise, so he suspected nothing when she, your daughter's therapist, came forward with 'proof' that he'd abused your daughter."

She finally stirred, shoving herself up to a sitting position and flinging the wash cloth across the room. "You can't prove any of this," she said.

"I've got a copy of Denise's therapy records with your daughter. I can prove the abuse claims were manufactured outside the counseling sessions."

"That's impossible."

"That's why people come to me. They think I can do things that are impossible for them, and I can."

"You've violated some law, I'm sure."

"I'm not much into 'you-violated-a-bigger-law-than-I-did' arguments. I'm not quite sure how many laws the two of you violated, let alone the number of ethical questions you've raised. But I do know when you found out your uncle died, the two of you threw your plan into action."

"If any of this were true, then why did I hire you to find my husband?"

"That's an easy one," I said. "Fear. Mark did the one thing you hadn't planned. He slipped all the bindings you had hog-tied him with. He left the law practice. He moved away. He disappeared. You lost your leverage and with that your security. You wanted to know where he was so he couldn't sneak up and surprise you."

She leaned forward slightly. "What do you want?"

Now we were in an arena she understood: certainly I, too, must be a blackmailer. I stood up and walked to the sofa to look down into her eyes. She held my gaze, her eyes flicking back and forth as she tried to see what I was thinking. "Nothing," I said.

Her eyes held steady. "Nothing?"

"I'm turning over all the information I have to Mark. What exactly he chooses to do with it, I don't know, but I can guess. I think you'll need to plan to give him half the money from your uncle's estate, since you were still married when you inherited it and he's entitled to half. And I suspect he'll want custody of your daughter, and he might even want Denise, at least, to get out of town. I don't think you need to worry about what I want; I think you need to worry about what he wants."

I opened the door to find my brave body guard catnapping on his feet. I turned back to see Margorie rushing to the telephone. I shut the door. I knew who she was calling, and I knew almost word for word what the panicked conversation would be.

I walked outside into the sunshine and headed down the sidewalk with my faithful cop driving seven paces behind. I didn't feel some great sense of victory or a flush of justice. I have never liked to see people in pain, even if they deserved it. Instead, I mouthed a silent warning in general: Don't come to me if you have something to hide. I am a two-edged sword.

THIRTY ONE

I'm sure I could make up all kinds of good excuses for my behavior, but I think cockiness was at the heart of it. I'd solved two tough cases this week, and I wanted to go for the grand slam. I could have let the police do their job, but I was getting impatient with their slowness. I decided to give them a little help.

I was sure Irwin was may man. I was so sure, I decided to stop by his house for a visit. I even called ahead to make sure he wasn't home.

Getting away alone was a little more difficult. I did have police protection, after all. Today, though, the police protection was upstairs helping Diane move some furniture around. Big, slow-witted cops are good for something, and those seemed to be the only kind they sent to protect me. I felt like I was doing the police department a favor: I was baby-sitting the cops they wanted to keep out of harm's way.

I left a note on the kitchen table saying I was going to a movie, which would fool only the cop and not Diane. She'd be mad at me, but she'd have to get in line behind Curry and Wilson. I won't offer any more excuses; sometimes computer people come in not-so-big, slow-witted packages, too.

***

Getting to Syzmoore's house was a bit of a trick. Not that he lived in a faraway place. In fact, if you went out his back gate, you could step into an alley that bisected his block, separating back yards from back yards. It was one of the features of this particular housing development. If you walked left down the alley, you'd come to a street. Across the street was an empty field with a sign on it that read FUTURE HOUSING DEVELOPMENT. If you crossed the field, you'd come to a road and across from that an alley just like the one behind Irwin's house. If you walked the length of that alley, you'd come to another road. Across that road was a combination park and playground. If you walked through the park, you could step into the back parking lot of Fremont High. Someone could easily take that journey at two in the morning and never be spotted.

I drove by Syzmoore's house first. The garage door was open and the car was gone. I then found a phone booth and called one more time. After that I found the alley. I drove my car down the alley and parked it behind Syzmoore's house. I did have a plan—I even stopped off at a store to get a few props. I was sure no one would buy it if I got caught, but I was only concerned about Irwin, not his neighbors.

I climbed out of my car and walked through his back gate. The house was a modest ranch style that looked in good repair, but the yard didn't look as good. Someone had done some spring planting, but it didn't look like anyone had cared for it since. The lawn needed mowing badly, and the flower beds were choked with weeds.

I circled the house with a clipboard in hand, making notations on the pad it held whenever I found something of interest. I circled the house twice. I was just getting ready to peer into a back window when a man stuck his head over the fence.

"Watcha doin' there?" he snapped out.

I glanced at him and made another notation on the clipboard. "Tax appraiser," I said.

"You gotta be putting me on. A taxman coming around on a Saturday night?"

I nodded in agreement. "You're telling me it's Saturday night. I'd rather be anyplace else, but I've got this one house left to do on this report, and I can't seem to ever catch anyone home." I could see a bit of doubt form in his eyes.

"You've got some credentials?"

"A pocket full of them," I said, reaching for my wallet. I paused and looked as sly as I could. "Say, you're not ..."

"Waterberry," he said.

"Right, Waterberry." I started thumbing through the sheets on the clipboard. "You know, I think you're scheduled for a new assessment next year, but as long as I'm out here ..."

"What are you talking about? You just go take care of Syzmoore and forget you ever saw me." His head disappeared behind the fence. From his yard he shouted out, "You're not going to find anyone home. The woman left for her sister's weeks ago. Syzmoore took off a couple of hours ago. Said he was goin' campin', then he was gonna catch up to the woman."

Irwin, the good science teacher that he was, was going to chase the flora and fauna for a while. Or he was going to run as fast as his little legs could carry him.

I moved around the house and peeked into each of the windows, making sure to write notes to keep the neighbors happy. From what I could see of the front room, the dining room and the kitchen, Irwin was very untidy indeed. He obviously had not had a woman to look after him for some time.

I saw the computer through the window of what must have originally been a bedroom. This was definitely Irwin's den. It was filled with stacks of books and magazines. On the one wall I could see clearly, just behind the computer, was a detailed map of the city.

One look at the computer told me that I didn't need to break in to crank it up. In the front of it was a gaping slot where a removable hard drive should have been. A smart man, Irwin, he knew that no one could prove much of anything with his computer without the hard drive. It also meant that if he got away with this, he'd only have to replace the hard drive and not the whole computer if he had to toss the drive.

When I got to the bathroom window, I realized Irwin no longer had it all together. I had to stand on a picnic bench to reach the small, frosted panel of glass. The window was nearly shut, but not quite. Standing on the bench I could see a thin gap I had not seen from the ground. I used a metal pen I had in my pocket to pry the window up enough for me to see through the gap.

Much more to my surprise than to hers, I stared at Mrs. Syzmoore in the bathtub. She wasn't taking a bath. In fact, she was fully clothed, and she had seen better days. I couldn't say for sure how long she had been dead because she was packed in dry ice.

I could just see Syzmoore showing up at an ice house almost daily to pick up dry ice. I'm sure he told them that he was a science teacher and easily convinced them he had an experiment of some kind in progress. The workers at the ice house would have stopped wondering after the second or third time.

"Say, I don't think you oughta be doin' that."

I damned near fell off the bench. "You're right," I said to the neighbor whose head was once again above the fence. "I think you should call the police."

"You don't stop lookin' in bathroom windows and I'll."

"No, Mr. Waterberry, I mean it. You need to call the police. There's a dead body in the bathroom."

Mr. Waterberry was stunned into silence for a moment. Finally, he mumbled, "You don't say. You don't say."

"I think it's Mrs. Syzmoore."

Waterberry's head nodded above the fence. "My wife said things weren't good between them. Neither one of us was surprised when she left."

"It doesn't look like she left."

"Oh," he said, softly. "Guess I'd better call the cops."

"Just a second," I said. I walked over to the fence and gave him one of my cards. "When they call, give them this. I've got some other business to take care of."

I wasn't anxious to spend the night here, explaining just exactly what I was doing. I liked it better when they came to my place and bullied me there.

I drove back feeling pretty smug. They'd have a tough time proving I wasn't right this time. I know they wanted to do it with good old police work, but they're the ones who hired me. And I delivered a killer. I was beginning to feel that my job, my company, might not have any limits to it except me. By the time I parked in my garage, I was ready to hire some more people and change the name of my firm to Dataman, Private Eye.

I walked into the building and passed the cop who was supposed to be guarding my door. "Hey, just a minute," I said.

He walked back to me. "Sorry," he said. "I was so happy to be getting off early I didn't even recognize you."

"Did they stop the guard on my door?"

"No, no, nothing like that. They sent my relief up early."

That was good news. I know that Irwin had packed up and left, but I wanted to make sure he wasn't going to take a parting shot at me before he left.

"Is Diane still in the apartment?"

"Oh, yes, she was making me a cup of coffee. I told her to invite the other fellow in for a cup instead of me."

"He's a uniformed officer?" I asked, feeling just a little uneasy.

"Oh, yeah. Different precinct, but a cop nonetheless."

"You do know him?"

"Can't say I do, but Portland is full of cops. We can't know them all."

I tried to relax. This was an experienced cop. If he didn't seem the least worried, there was no reason for me to be. I expected to see a lot of cops before the evening was out. Still, Irwin had been clever ...

"Thanks," I said and headed upstairs.

THIRTY TWO

I don't know what I expected to find when I opened the door to my apartment. I guess, in the back of my head, I didn't expect Syzmoore to simply pack up and leave town. I swung the door open cautiously. What I found was Diane serving a cop a cup of coffee. He was several sizes too big to be Irwin.

Diane got up and came over to give me a hug. She backed up a step with her hands on my hips and said, "You've been a very bad boy. You lied to me."

I never liked opened-ended statements that said you lied. They made me want to confess to every lie I had ever told. "Just exactly which lie are we talking about?" I asked.

"You mean there's been more than one?"

"That depends on how far back you want to go."

"The one about the movie," she said.

"I got an urge to drive."

"I got a call from Wilson. He said under no circumstances were you to leave your office once you returned. Eventually, he said, there would be a number of people here to be very rude to you."

"Were those his exact words?"

"No, but I won't use his exact words. I'm too much of a lady."

"I do know you're a lot of woman, even if you are too much of a lady."

"What did you find that has the lieutenant so upset?"

"A killer and a dead body."

She took me by the hand. "You come over here, sit down and tell us all about it. Maybe the presence of this nice policeman will keep me from hurting you."

I told the two of them what I had seen at Irwin's Syzmoore's place. I felt that should wrap up the case, I said.

The cop, Jerry Mathews, one of those good-looking, curly-haired, muscle men in uniform, shrugged. "I know a detective who always says it ain't over until it's over."

"I've heard that said of sports," I offered.

"If murder's a sport. Investigations sometimes take some twists and turns. The guy you were sure did it in the beginning, didn't have a thing to do with it in the end. Maybe Irwin killed his wife. Maybe she died of natural causes and he just can't stand to let her go. Maybe he shoots taggers. Maybe his wife did and he finally decided to stop her."

I had to look at him hard to see if he was serious. He drank his coffee and munched on some cookies that Diane had put on the table. I didn't see a sign that he was kidding. He really did think there was a possibility that Irwin hadn't done it.

"Look," I said. "Irwin's kind of a meek guy. Kids have been pushing him around for years. A new principal comes in. She tells him to shape up his act. Some students tag his desk tops. He gets put on a plan of assistance, which means he could lose his job. His wife finally tires of being married to a mouse. She says she's going to leave him. The man's been wound tight for years. Suddenly he's been cranked a notch too tight. The spring snaps. He kills his wife. He goes after taggers, symbols of what got him into all this trouble in the first place."

"Sounds good to me," Jerry said.

"Thanks."

"Only I would have gone for the principal after the wife."

"Yeah, well, he wasn't thinking straight at the time."

"No one will know for sure until they get the guy."

I was getting really tired of people punching holes in my theory. I was the only one who had a clue about what was going on. I found a body they hadn't found. I wanted some respect.

I didn't get it just then. Instead an all-too-familiar sound of my window being punched out was followed by Jerry taking a dive to the floor. I didn't wait. I lunged at Diane and knocked her to the floor, too.

Jerry was rolling slowly back and forth. He'd taken part of the slug. More glass was punched out. A bullet plowed up splinters from the floor about a foot from me. I hadn't thought to close the blinds.

I pushed Diane's butt. "Move as fast as you can into the kitchen and stay behind the counter." She did as she was told. I crawled under the table and hugged the wall low. When I was close to the kitchen door, I lunged back and grabbed Jerry's collar. I damned near pulled every muscle in my body, but I did manage to drag him into the kitchen with me.

I grabbed some towels out of a drawer and had Diane put a compress on Jerry's shoulder to stop the bleeding. Once we'd done all we could, I looked around for the phone. It was in the other room, on the coffee table.

"Jerry," I said. "I need to call for help. You must have something on you for that."

He curled his left hand and used a finger to point toward his shoulder. "Turn on the mike."

On his left shoulder was small, square microphone with a switch on the bottom. I clicked it the other way and the mike crackled.

"What do I do now?" I asked.

"As long as I'm down, just talk."

"This is Tom Walkinshaw. I'm at my home. We are being shot at from the parking garage across the way. A police officer has been hit. We need immediate help."

Jerry wasn't going to be of much help. He passed out. I couldn't say that I blamed him. I'd been in the same position not that long ago. I unsnapped his automatic and removed it from the holster.

"Do you know how to use one of those?" Diane asked.

"I know enough to make sure you don't have any of your body parts in the way before you pull the trigger."

"Just make sure you don't have any of mine in the way, either."

I checked to see that the safety was off. Good sense told me I should wait here for the police to arrive. Good sense makes life boring. I said to Diane, "I'm going to make sure the front door is unlocked. I don't want the cops breaking it down when they get here."

"Why don't you wait until they start pounding on it?"

"Because that would be the smart thing to do, and then I'd lose my front door."

I reached out and pushed open the door into my office. Nothing happened. I then did a rather graceful, head-first dive into the next room, sliding across the oak flooring until I was stopped by a table leg. The leg stopped me, but the gun kept going.

I crawled in the dim light toward the gun. I didn't get very far. A pair of legs suddenly appeared in the way. I looked up into the barrel of a revolver. "Irwin, is that you?"

"Yes, Tom, it sure is." He had a soft voice with a slight drawl to it. He didn't sound like someone who'd killed a dozen or more people. The window for the cat was open wide. While we were taking care of Jerry, Irwin had hurried over, probably pulled the fire escape ladder down, scooted along the ledge, and climbed through the window. Agile little guy, considering his age.

I sat back on my haunches. "I'm sure glad it's you, Irwin. People keep trying to convince me I'm wrong. Nothing personal, but I'm glad I wasn't."

"I think we need to leave here, Tom."

I got up slowly and started toward the outside door. "I'm all yours," I said.

"We'll need the girl, too, Tom. Call her."

That was the one thing I didn't want to do. I hoped Diane had locked herself in the bathroom by now. "Let's just keep this between us," I said. "That's how we've played the game so far."

"There's no fun in winning if the losers aren't made to suffer. Get the girl or I'll kill you now, and then go in and kill her."

"Diane," I called. "Lock yourself in the bathroom, now!"

She stepped through the open doorway. Now was not the time to ignore directions. "Hello Irwin," she said. "You've had a tough last couple of weeks, haven't you?"

Irwin wasn't in the mood for talking. He herded us together, and then he retrieved the gun I'd dropped. He had me open the door and check outside, and then he forced us into the hallway. "We're going to the roof," he said.

"Been there, done that," I said. "Besides, there's nothing to see up there at this time of night."

Irwin didn't have a sense of humor. I was a bit surprised that I did, at least at this moment. Hey, but if you can't joke when you're terrified, when can you?

Diane seemed to be handling it pretty well. She was no more pale than I was, and she hadn't wet her pants, either. At one point she took my hand and squeezed it. If I was mad at her for not locking herself in the bathroom, I forgave her then.

"Just think," I said, "if you'd locked yourself in the bathroom, you would've missed all this."

"If I'd locked myself in the bathroom, he'd have killed you and then come after me. Besides, the lock on your bathroom door doesn't work, stupid."

"Oh yeah, I forgot." She lost a few points with me for bravery, but got a few extra for good sense.

"What are we going to do on the roof, Irwin?" I asked.

"I'm going to kill you, and then I'm going to escape."

He said it kind of like, "Turn to page three twenty-three and read chapter ten."

"Any particular reason why you want to kill me?"

"Yes. You didn't follow directions."

Oops. I knew I'd done something wrong in all this. "Which directions were those?"

"I told you that if you didn't stop trying to catch me you would die."

"Wait a minute," I said. "Don't I get any points for catching you? That ought to count for something."

"I think you're confused about who has the gun."

I wasn't confused about that at all. We were climbing the last set of stairs to the top floor. I glanced back to see if I might whirl around quickly and leap down on top of Irwin. He must have given that some thought. He stayed well back. If I leaped, he could shoot me about six times before I got to him. You can't fool a science teacher about physics.

"Why didn't you just shoot us back there?"

"The police will be here at any second. It'll take them a

while to think of the roof. Long enough for me to kill the two of you and leave."

"Where's a guy go after he kills a couple of more people and can't go home again?"

"I've hiked and camped for years. I'll disappear into the woods and never be heard of again."

That was the first time I heard a hint of excitement in his voice. Until then everything had been flat. The man was burned out inside. I didn't know how to deal with that.

"What's the point in killing us?"

"You need to be punished. Killing her first will be even more punishment. Besides, if I let you live, you'd find me."

"Can I get your endorsement? You'll be great for my business."

"In a few minutes, you'll be out of business."

We stopped in front of the door to the roof. "Open it," he said.

I checked my pockets. "Darn. I seem to have left my keys in the apartment."

The gun cocked. "Okay. I'll kill you here."

He wasn't much for bluffs. "Wait! I think I just found them."

When we reached the roof, Diane decided to step in. "We have a few minutes. Do you want to talk about it?"

I didn't even have to look over the side of the building to know that a dozen police cars were below. I could see their lights reflecting off the buildings. And more sirens could be heard in the distance. Sure, he had lots of time.

"When she found out I'd been put on a plan of assistance, she decided she wanted a divorce. I didn't believe her at first—until I found out she'd filed. We argued. I strangled her. It felt good. The ones after that felt better."

That certainly was to the point. What do you do with the next fifty-eight minutes of your counseling session, doctor? "You'll regret killing us," I said. "You won't feel good about it at all."

This wasn't one of your luxury roofs. It was covered with old tar paper and pigeon droppings. Diane suggested we could build a deck up her, add some potted trees and flowers, buy some lawn furniture and get a barbecue. That would be nice, I said, and then those, too, could be covered in pigeon droppings. The roof did not give me romantic notions. Nor was it a place where I wanted to die.

I took a step toward Irwin and said, "Let's reconsider our options." That's when he shot me in the thigh. I dropped to the roof and rolled around in the pigeon poop, trying somehow to stop the incredible pain. "Goddamn it, Irwin," I moaned, "you're a science experiment gone bad."

"Come back here," Irwin ordered.

I hadn't gone anyplace to come back from. "I'm still down here, Irwin." It was then that I realized he was talking to Diane. While he was busy shooting me, she'd leaped into the darkness and disappeared behind the mechanics that sprouted up all over the roof. Good for her.

"I'll kill him now and then come and get you."

"I'm sure the police heard the gun shot, Irwin," Diane's calm voice said from the shadows. "You might kill him, but I don't think you'll get to me in time."

That was a little self-centered, I thought, but good thinking. To make things interesting, I pulled off one of my shoes and tossed it behind Irwin. He turned toward the noise. I got up in my best three-point stance and hopped off in the other direction.

Irwin turned and shot. He wasn't any better shooting at moving targets with a pistol than he was with a rifle.

When he crossed into a beam of light, I could see that he had a slight look of pique on his face. The talking was done. Now he was on the way to kill us both. I took off my other shoe and waited. When he was close enough, I let it fly.

It must have come out of the dark, because he made no attempt to dodge it. The shoe hit him square in the face. I'd have laughed, but he recovered very quickly and kept moving in my direction. Something clattered to his right. Diane was at work on the other side of the roof.

He wasn't much into diversions. He ignored the noise and kept coming. This time a noise came from the left. He turned to it, because that's where the fire escape was. He fired at something moving by fast. It was Buck. The little beggar made a clean get away, disappearing down the fire escape.

"You can kill me, Irwin, but my cat will stalk you to the end of the world and take his revenge."

You'll have to think of your own clever things to say when someone is out to kill you. But damned if I was going to let him think I was taking this seriously. He might kill me, but I still hoped to rob him of the satisfaction of it.

I had another idea. I shouted, "He's got a revolver from which he has fired at least three shots! He also has a cop's automatic! I don't think he has any other weapons! Right now you've got a clear shot at him!"

"Shut up," he said. He moved quickly in the direction of my voice. "Just shut up."

"He's closing in on me! Do it now!" I shouted.

I could see him in the dim light. He paused, looking all around, trying to see the cops he thought I could see. I just wished I could see some cops.

"Kill him, guys! He's not going to go peacefully."

His head snapped forward. I saw one of Diane's shoes fly off into space. He turned and fired in her direction. I was out and hopping in much more than a flash. I timed it all wrong. He had more than enough time to turn back in my direction and aim the gun at my head. Another shoe flew out of the darkness and hit him in the shoulder. The bullet nicked my left ear. I was still alive when I hobbled right over the top of him.

I'd forgotten how small he was. I was sprawled in more pigeon shit and he was scrambling to his feet behind me. I heard the gun go off just as I felt the whole back of my head go numb.

Talk about thick skulls, I thought. I just got shot in the head and I could still hear, albeit my ears were ringing. Blood was running down my neck and down the side of my face.

I'm not dead, I thought, but he must think I'm dead, so I think maybe I'll just play dead. That was a good idea until I heard Diane scream.

I crawled to him on hands and knees, and then got to my feet. Nothing in my body was any too sharp, including the pain in my leg. The blow to my head must have done something to numb the pain. I could even walk, although that was a trick when I was seeing everything in double. Irwin had Diane trapped in the corner of the building. I could hear him saying to her, "... and when women went to work, that was the beginning of the end. They have ruined the world."

He certainly was a hostile little man with a lot of archaic ideas. I walked up behind him. He would probably never have known I was there if it hadn't been for the look on Diane's face. It's tough to squeeze out horror and relief both at the same time. Irwin turned around to see what it was.

I suppose I could have done something else, but I really was tired of being shot by this guy. I stepped into him before he could get the gun around, grabbed him in a bear hug, and then—don't try this at home—I carried him the few feet and threw him over the edge of the building. He made a little wimp of a science teacher noise on the way down and made a thud that would behoove a much smaller person. The gun made a bigger noise when it hit the ground. Maybe I'm prejudiced. Maybe he made more noise than that.

"Sorry about that, Diane," I said, "but a guy can get shot only so many times ..." I sank down to the roof to cover whatever few spots I had left that didn't have pigeon shit on them. "By the way, I love you." Then I passed out.

THIRTY THREE

I am not dead. That has come as a surprise to a lot of people, including Diane, who saw me get shot in the back of the head from close range.

In the end, Irwin went out the way he came in. He started out not being a very good teacher, he ended up not being a very good killer. He, too, was surprised to find me alive. I saw it in his eyes just before I threw him off the building.

I'll give him credit for trying. He did shoot me in the leg, but, of course, he missed the bone or I wouldn't have been able to get up that last time. And he did try to shoot me in the head, but Diane's shoe made a difference and the bullet only creased my earlobe. He was a little more successful when he tried to shoot me in the head the second time.

Unfortunately physics caught up with him. The angle was just a little bit off. Instead of caving in the back of my head, the bullet slid around between my skull and my scalp and exited just over my right ear. He was pretty stunned to see me coming after him again. Everyone else he shot in the head stayed dead.

In the hospital, I asked the doctor if I might come out of this with a romantic scar to show the world. He said that in a few years when I started to go bald I'd have a lot of scars to show the world. I hope he was kidding about going bald.

The newspapers said Diane's quick thinking was the reason we survived. Diane credits me for saving our lives. I said it was Buck. He made a hell of move just at the right moment. I even threw out his dried cat food and started getting him canned stuff.

The story made the news all the way down to California. My kids read in the papers that their dad caught a murderer. They're coming up next weekend for a visit. Diane has decided to stay at the Vintage Plaza for those nights when the kids are here. She says she's looking forward to going to bed without climbing a ladder. In truth, she says she wants to make a good impression on the kids. She's afraid if they find us living together, it'll start us all off on the wrong foot.

I'm not complaining. I know she wants to make a good impression because she plans to be around for a long time. She knows she'll be seeing them again down the road, and she wants to start building a good foundation with them.

I haven't gotten any gracious thanks from the police. Wilson called one day while I was in the hospital and said, "You know, you should be dead. Any time you start thinking you're a hero, just remember that."

Curry waited until I got home before he called. He wanted to remind me that I still needed to write up a final report and that he really liked the nifty covers I put them in. He did say he thought the police would use my services again, as long as I promised not to play private investigator.

Let me see. I only got shot four times on this case. I wondered if that was going to be above or below average each time the cops came calling. Diane says that if they come calling again, I am not home.

Right now I'm curled up in bed. Diane and I are enjoying being able to snuggle since we almost lost the chance to do it again. Oh, yeah, Buck is wedged between us, stretched out on his back and purring.

Life's pretty damned good.